The Monster She Trusted

—·—

R. L. Bates

First Edition October 2022

Cataloging-in-Publication data is on file with the Library of Congress, and available upon request.

LCCN: 2022917584

ISBN 979-8-9868917-0-5 (pbk)

ISBN 979-8-9868917-1-2 (hc)

Contents

For the Em to my Hunter.
Thank you for everything.

"If all else perished, and he remained, I should still continue to be."

— Emily Brontë, *Wuthering Heights*

PROLOGUE

Note to Self:
　　Things to remember. . .
　　　　1. Always trust your gut.

　　　　2. When you think you're home free, you're not.

ONE

— • —

MADELEINE: HAVE YOU HEARD FROM ABI?

ME: I JUST WOKE UP, SO, NO. NOT SINCE LAST NIGHT. WHY?

MADELEINE: SHE AND DAD GOT INTO IT LAST NIGHT, AND SHE LEFT. DIDN'T COME BACK.

ME: SOMETIMES SHE GOES TO STUDY IN THE MORNINGS.

MADELEINE: BED HASN'T BEEN SLEPT IN, NO NEW TOWEL FROM A SHOWER, AND NO DISHES IN THE SINK.

ME: HMM, ALRIGHT. I'LL SHOOT HER A TEXT.

MADELEINE: THANKS.

Two

—◆—

Days since Abi's disappearance: 1
A knock echoes off the living room walls.

"I'll get it," Em says as she sets her book open and face down on the coffee table. Once unraveled from her blanket, she pushes off the couch and heads toward the front door. There's a pause, then a scoff. "To what do we owe the pleasure?"

"Is there a Hunter Greene here?" says a male with a deep voice.

I don't need to see who's there to know.

Cops. Great.

Bakersfield isn't what you'd call upper class — hell, it's not even middle class. It's a little town outside of a big city that houses the struggling, working class. For reasons I don't particularly feel like getting into right now, we've come to distrust a handful of labels, and, unfortunately, cops are one of them.

"Depends. Why'a askin'?" The sound of her foot shifting on the hardwood tells me she's adjusted her weight to one hip, the typical stance she takes when an attitude is brewing. Em has always had dry humor, and while I don't think it's a bad thing, it's not something that bodes well with those pesky civil servants.

"*Dios mío*, Em..." I stand from the couch with an exasperated sigh. "...They're just doing their job." As I approach the door, she peers over her shoulder, blows a raspberry, and moves out of my way.

"Killjoy," she mumbles, and meanders back to the couch.

The air wafting in is cooler than I expect, and sends a chill through me causing a small shudder. Early October isn't usually a time of the year that requires heavier clothing, but, apparently, we'll be having a harsh winter. I hate the cold. I'm not built for it.

Can we hurry this up? I don't feel like freezing just so you can ask some stupid questions.

I look between the two officers for a moment. Males. Tall but not intimidating. I do my best to put on a decent smile, but it's awkward and doesn't reach my eyes. "What can I do for you?"

"I'm Officer Samson; this is Officer Hughes. Do you have time to talk?" asks the owner of the deep voice.

I hate the way he asks that, and I hate even more that I can't read his expression. The events from the last few days roll through my mind: no tickets, no stop signs or red lights were run, and Em hasn't broken into an abandoned building *this week*.

"Uh, sure." I gesture for them to take a couple of steps back, and join them on the porch after closing the door. "What's this about?" I cross my arms when a gust of wind picks up.

I should've brought a hoodie with me.

"You're familiar with an Abigail Perkins, is that correct?" asks Officer Samson.

So, this is about Abi? Crap. What happened?

"Yes."

Why do you want to know?

"And she's your girlfriend?" There's a stiffness building in his questions. From my experience, this usually means the person doesn't like the way their questions are being answered.

"Yes."

"How long have you been dating?" Officer Samson gestures for his partner to start taking notes.

"It'll be three years this coming Valentine's Day," I say. The more they ask questions, the more a knot in my stomach starts to tighten. This whole situation feels too similar to what happened two years ago, except now I'm in Mom's place.

"Aw, how cute. Have you heard from her?" Officer Hughes asks while looking up from a pocket-sized notepad. He clears his throat, glances down at what he's written, then back to me.

You look uncomfortable.

"When was the last time you heard from her, I should say?"

I stare at Officer Hughes, blank-faced, and raise an eyebrow.

Are you new?

"Last night." My attention turns back to Officer Samson. I like him more — probably because he's not trying to find a common ground or make himself appear like a friend. He's direct, and while the questioning isn't fun, I respect it. "She texted me that she'd made it home safe after studying at the library and that she got an acceptance letter from BCC."

"Bakersfield Community College? It's pretty early for the fall semester acceptances, isn't it?" Officer Samson offers a smile, and while it appears friendly and sincere, there's a part of me that has a feeling he's doing it to try and get me to open up more. That's always their aim, isn't it? Get the person comfortable, make them trust you, and then see what they offer on their own without coaxing.

Those mind games don't work on me, dude. Sorry.

"She applied over the summer for the winter semester, and acceptance letters started going out last week. She wanted to take a course or two before fully starting next fall."

"Full senior course load along with a couple college classes. Ambitious girl."

I nod.

"And, you haven't heard from her since last night?" asks Officer Samson.

"No."

"Not at all?" He glances at Officer Hughes, and a silent conversation moves between them before he looks back at me. Watching this causes a shiver has nothing to do with the weather. "Is that unusual?"

What's going on?

"Yeah, I guess. We always meet on the football field before homeroom to say hi and walk in together. When she didn't show, I figured she was taking a mental health day." That last part was a half-truth. If there's one thing I've learned throughout my life, it's to keep some details to yourself until you know what you're dealing with. Since they're not telling me what's going on, I'll keep certain things quiet for now. "Is there something I should be aware of? Is Abi okay?"

"Just a routine check. We're sure she's fine. If you hear from her, give me a call." Officer Samson hands me his card.

Does this mean she didn't come home? Did her dad report her missing?

Note to self: text Maddi.

"Yeah, of course," I say in my most convincing tone.

I wave as they get back in the car. Once they're completely out of sight, I go back inside where a wash of sudden warmth causes goosebumps to spread up my arms.

Until now, I thought she was taking time for herself. Sure, it doesn't usually mean she ignores her phone, but when big fights happen, sometimes Abi isolates. I've seen some serious stuff go down in the Perkinses home, and while their father has never been physically abusive, it doesn't stop him from shouting and screaming and running the household with fear. When he gets mad enough, he's tyrannical.

"What was all that about?" Em asks. At one point during my time outside, she'd pulled her hair into a messy bun on the top of her head, making the ends of her hair splay out in random directions at the crown of her head. Her eyes are fixated on her book — *The Exorcist* — despite the question being directed at me. One thing about Em is she loves dark and spooky. If something is horror- or crime-themed, she's all over it.

"They were asking questions about Abi." I pull out my phone and take a seat next to her.

She sets the book down again and studies me with her eyebrows pressed together. "Is she okay?"

That's cute, you're showing concern for Abi.

Em's my twin sister and with that comes a certain level of attachment. Most people say we're connected at the hip, but it's more than that. We're each other's best friend, soulmate. Growing up, you couldn't have one without the other, a tendency that never went away. Because of this, Em and Abi spend a lot of time with each other. They've never been super close, but when you're around someone enough, you're bound to form some kind of friendship.

"I assumed so. According to Maddi, she and their dad got into it last night, and she went off somewhere. I texted her this morning, but she never answered."

"Hmm." I can see the gears turning in her head. In another life, Em was a detective. I hate watching whodunit movies and shows with her because she always calls who the killer will be within the first fifteen minutes.

"She didn't meet me before school, but I figured she was probably taking a day away, y'know?" My thread with Abi immediately pulls up when I unlock my phone.

Me: Hey, Maddi's worried about you. You OK?

Me: I brought coffee for you <3

Me: Heading to class. Love you, hope to see you in English.

I dial her number and put the phone to my ear. She still has one of those services that lets you program a song to play for the caller while your phone rings. This month it's a song about having the eye of a tiger. When the automated voice comes on telling me to leave a message, I close my eyes and pause, waiting for the beep. "Hey, babe, it's me. The cops came by asking questions. Can I get a sign of life? It's going to be okay. It'll work itself out, I promise.

Call me back. Love you." I hang up the phone, lips pressing into a thin line, and exhale heavily through my nose.

"What's there to work out?" Em asks.

You never pry this much. Don't tell me you're getting flashback feelings too...

"Remember that talk Mom and Dad had with us about the benefits of community college a few years ago?"

She nods.

"I told Abi about it, and she said it sounded like a good idea and would be interested in doing something like that too. It was partially so we could stay close for another couple of years, but also to save the money. Ever since her dad found out she decided to go to BCC, he's been saying she's throwing her life away." I scoff. "It only got worse when he found out *I* was one of the reasons. They want her to apply to an Ivy League."

"That's stupid. There's no shame in the community college game."

"I'm aware, thanks, Captain Obvious." I smirk, and the quip earns me a punch to my arm. When I move to return it, Em dodges and sticks her tongue out at me.

"You know what I mean," she says. "It's her life. Let her do what she wants."

"That's what I said."

THREE

Days since Abi's disappearance: 8

Over the next week, things go from bad to worse. There's absolutely no sign of Abi. Anywhere. The day after the cops stopped by, I tried calling her several times, but her phone was either turned off or died because the voicemail stopped accepting new messages halfway through the day and then stopped ringing altogether. I feel like I'm going crazy. While there have been times that Abi and I didn't talk much or we gave each other space, in a normal, day-to-day setting, we're in almost constant communication. I'm known for sending her silly or stupid pictures I find on the internet or doodles I make in the middle of class while she's usually the one sending back a reactionary photo or telling me that I should be paying attention to what's being taught.

Questions and what-ifs constantly tumble around my head. Calling them intrusive is an understatement. Where is my girlfriend? Why isn't she answering the phone? Why isn't her phone on? It's all I can focus on, even during school hours. For some context, I'm a good student. I have a 4.0, even though almost no one believes it, and I'm waiting to find out if I've been selected for admission to BCC next year. So, me, distracted at school? It's a big deal.

Every time I try calling Officer Samson about the case, I'm told, "Sorry, kid, we can't disclose information on an open investigation."

What a typical response.

Mr. Perkins is no better. On day four of Abi being missing, I try to go by the house and am immediately met with aggression and a tirade of reasons about why Abi being missing is my fault. They had a whole plan for her before she met me, and according to him, I ruined it. Blaming me for these things is crap, by the way. Of course, Abi wants to go to college and have a better life, but she isn't blind to the fact that there are multiple ways to achieve that. Not to mention, I don't cause the fights at home. I didn't create the plan for an Ivy League education and convince Abi that the only way to have a good life is to start with thousands of dollars of debt. I support her, what she wants to do, and explain the options available to her. The day the school started talking to us about our futures and what we want or what college we are planning on going to, we sat down and discussed things. We're building a plan for a better life. Together. The fact that it's a plan including me is beside the point.

People always tell us we're "end game," whatever that means, and that we're going to "make it." It's a little surprising to hear. At first, she was constantly asked why she's with someone like me — a "hoodlum from a lowlife family" — which only forced me to work toward being accepted by her father. To hell with the rest of the world, but at the very least, I wanted her father to like me. I got there, eventually, but it took time. In reality, neither of our families are better off than the other, but there's a certain level of prejudice that gets thrown at you when you're not in the majority, if you know what I mean.

In addition to the way the outside world sees us, there are the personality differences. Abi is artsy and whimsical and imaginative. I'm... not. Where Abi looks at the brighter side of life and expects everything to fall into place, I'm logical and realistic. She's smart and beautiful and talented. She sees the allure in the night sky and imagines what worlds might be out there; all I see are hot balls of gas and the probability that while there might be life on some distant planet, we'll never see it in our lifetime. She always talks about wanting to become an artist and writer after college. She's my opposite in so many ways, and it's one of the things I love the most about her.

Maddi and I have kept in contact with each other almost daily after the visit from the cops. She says it's important for us to be there for each other. I think it's more for her benefit than mine. When things get hard, I recoil into my little corner and deal with things alone, almost never asking for help. Maddi isn't like that. She's a talker and expressive to an almost irritating degree. When something happens, she has to talk through it to fully process, and if she's not able to, she'll fixate until she can. It's caused issues with her and Abi on more than one occasion. It's never fun being stuck between the two of them during those instances. Trust me.

I receive small updates now and again — mostly what Maddi is able to overhear when her father talks to Officer Samson — but nothing major. They still have no leads, they have no suspects, and if there isn't anything to go on, there isn't any way to move forward.

MADELEINE: NEED YOU. NERO'S. ASAP!

When the text message comes in, the world feels like it's closing in, and my stomach threatens to send everything I ate this morning back to the surface. All the questions from the past week swirl around again with a new one tacked on to the end: was she found?

ME: 10 MINUTES.

I'm not sure what's going to come of this meeting — or why it's being called at all — but if Maddi doesn't want to say it over the phone, it's serious.

"I'll be back later, mom!" I pull on a jacket and my boots, then grab the car keys and I'm out the door. Mom shouts something after me, but I can't make it out and there isn't time to turn around.

Normally, Mom gives us the third degree about where we're going and with who — it's a safety thing after what happened with Dad. I'll text her when I get to Nero's. Right now, I need to get to Maddi and see what's going on.

Maybe Abi's finally home.

FOUR

Days since Abi's disappearance: 8

Nero's Café is the only place in town that can manage a decent cup of coffee. We've got other places like The Cyber Café and George's Place, but if you're hoping for quality, Nero's is the way to go. It's a cute little set up. It's one of those places with exposed brick and murals painted on the walls from local artists. Very artisan, apparently. I've never really understood what that meant. What I do know is it reminds me of the kind of place that pretentious hipsters sit in to be seen as important while they write their insignificant screenplays and convince themselves they're going to create the next great intellectual tome to inspire a generation.

Once inside, I pull out my phone, send a text to Mom apologizing for leaving so quickly with a promise that I'll explain everything later, and slide it back into my pocket before looking around. It's not busy today. A few scattered tables are occupied, and there are people with laptops out or headphones in while they read, but for the most part, it's unpopulated.

Good. At least it won't be loud.

That's one of the most annoying things in the world: to try and have a serious conversation in a bustling place.

Maddi's sitting in her normal spot — inside, off to the right, by the window — but it takes me a minute to recognize her. For a girl that's normally so well put together, it looks like she hasn't slept in weeks and hasn't eaten in even longer. She's engulfed in a large hoodie and sweatpants, something I've never seen her wear out of the house before, and her hair is pulled into a tight ponytail with week-old grease at the roots. She has dark circles forming under her eyes that make her appear years older than she is, and her normal, perfectly constructed eyeliner is missing. Maddi insists on doing her makeup when she's going out so seeing her like this feels wrong and only drives home the gravity of the situation.

This is really doing a number on you.

"Hey," I say to get her attention.

"Hey, where's Em?" Her eyes glance passed me, searching, then back.

"Cai wanted to take her to breakfast."

"Oh." She seems disappointed but does her best to hide it by looking down at her mug.

That was an interesting reaction.

"I was going to order for you, but I couldn't remember if you liked tea or coffee." She's fidgety, and, based on the fact that her mug seems barely touched, I assume it has to do with whatever she called me here for.

I sit down across from her. "It's fine, thanks for the thought. For the record, coffee. Always coffee."

For the most part, studying Maddi to figure out what she's thinking is like rereading a book for the thousandth time — the girl is more transparent than a pane of glass. The opposite of Abi in that way.

Whatever is going on is making her anxious. She's tapping her mug with her nails and bouncing her leg so quickly it looks like she's vibrating. The longer the clinking sound goes on, the more it makes me want to scream. I try to give her a few more moments of silence before finally drawing in a deep breath. I understand all of this is stressful for her, but she called me here and now she's avoiding the topic entirely.

This is stressful to me too.

"Madeleine, *speak*. What the hell is going on?" Em's voice runs through my head: *Don't be a douche.*

And there it is — the waterworks. Tears fall down her cheeks so rapidly, I'm worried she'll overflow her mug if she tilts her head forward. I watch the streams create little rivers down her cheeks and neck, then start to soak the front of her hoodie. "Hunter... oh God. I tried. You need to know I tried."

Oh... Oh no.

"I need you to believe that I told them to keep looking and not to give up. They wouldn't listen. I don't know what to do," she says, trying to hold back a sob that chokes her in protest. I can barely understand Em when she does her excited rambles, and she's my sister. Understanding Maddi through her sobs is nearly impossible.

Okay, wait, so she hasn't been found?

"They aren't going to do anything. And th-they keep saying because she's almost eighteen and because she's run away before, that that's all this is. They believe she's using it as a scare tactic toward my dad because he's upset with her about the college thing and they're... they're...." She can't even finish her words before succumbing to sobs again.

I sit in silence for several moments looking anywhere but at her. Part of the whole *isolating when upset* thing means I don't cry often, and I sure as hell don't do it in *public*. It makes me extremely uncomfortable when others cry, but in this kind of situation I'm supposed to try to console her, right?

"Maddi," I say in a stiff tone. She looks at me with a sniffle. Watching her like this pulls at something in my chest, but I'm at a loss of what to say. Am I supposed to reminder her that it'll be okay? That *she* will be okay? No one knows that. Do I tell her that they'll find Abi? Clearly, they're not searching anymore.

I'm so bad at this.

"Yeah?" Her hands wrap around her mug. She's desperate for security, and that mug is her safety blanket.

"Just to recap; Abi *hasn't* been found. They don't have a clue on where she is, but they're going to *stop* looking for her because they think she's decided to run away?" I try to keep my tone as soft and understanding as possible, but the scrunch of her eyebrows tells me I'm failing.

A nod accompanies the slowing of her tears. "Yeah," she says, then stares down at her cup again. "I tried to tell them to keep going, but one officer — Officer Hughes, I think? — said something about it not being a high-priority case." Her voice shakes, and it's becoming more and more obvious she thinks this is her fault somehow.

Note to self: Officer Hughes not only tries too hard but is also insensitive.

I'm not sure if I'm upset because of their decision to give up on Abi or because it's starting to feel like something else is wrong, but we don't need anyone freaking out or getting ahead of themselves. I reach across the table and take one of her hands in an attempt to try and distract her. "She's going to turn up, okay?"

"How, Hunter?" She pulls her hand from mine and wipes her cheeks, but more tears immediately replace them.

Please stop crying.

"How is she going to just *turn up*? Are we supposed to wait for her to walk through the door one day? Expect her to get herself out of whatever situation she's in? You know this isn't my sister. You know she doesn't disappear like this. You know—"

"*Stop.*" The stiffness in my voice is back, and this time it's accompanying the annoyance and anxiety bubbling under the surface. When I see her bottom lip quiver, I pause and take a moment to breathe. The Greenes have a reputation for their quick tempers and I might as well be the spokesperson. "Breathe, okay? I need you to breathe. No one is saying that Abi will randomly walk into the house. I think we've already established that's probably not going to happen, but sitting here freaking out isn't going to help either." Silence settles between us. "Okay?"

She nods.

"Good, okay. So, if the police aren't going to put effort into finding her, then we will."

Maddi scoffs, then looks toward the window and takes a sip of her drink. Abi does the same thing when she's trying to figure out what to say next. That thought causes a new wave of pain, but I keep it from my face. "You really think that *we* can find her? The cops couldn't find anything. What are two teenagers going to be able to do?" The sarcasm in her voice seems to override the desire to cry. "We don't have their resources or anything like that."

It's my turn to scoff now, earning me a pointed look.

Man, you're like a clone of Abi when you do that.

"Listen, the cops obviously don't have many resources anyway. At least if we find something, we can do it our way. Think about it. If we need to get into someone's house and they're a student, we befriend that student and have them invite us over. We can sneak into places and ask around without making people paranoid." Someone at a neighboring table clears their throat, reminding me that we're in a public place talking about potential breaking-and-entering scenarios. I glance over in the direction the sound came from and do a double take.

Mr. Clarke? Ms. Johnson? Mr. Richards?

It's always so weird to see teachers outside of school. It's like seeing a wild animal walking around the city or a cat on its hind legs. You know it can happen, they're part of the community after all, but you're still never prepared for it. I prefer teachers when they're an entity that doesn't leave the halls of the school.

Mr. Clarke is the senior English teacher and Abi's favorite. Despite her shining words about him, I've rarely had the same experience. He's always marked me down or been harsher on my work than others. I remember a time Em and I tested it by swapping our names on a book report. Surprise, surprise, Em got a higher grade than me. We confronted him about it, and he lightened up some. I probably could've gone to the principal or school board, but would they believe me?

Debatable.

Ms. Johnson is the school librarian. She's another one that Abi has a glowing recommendation for, and while she's nicer than Mr. Clarke, she's still not part of my fan club. To be fair, I probably wouldn't be either if I constantly had to shush someone when they were around. I can be respectful, but that doesn't mean I'm quiet. Mr. Richards, on the other hand? The guy loves me. He's the gym teacher and basketball coach, and has been scouting me for the team since he saw me play in gym freshman year. I'm good, don't get me wrong, but basketball isn't something I want to make *my thing*. I'll play it around the neighborhood with friends, but when it comes to a true hobby, I'm all about boxing.

Despite the obviously pointed looks from the trio, I offer Mr. Clarke a small, forced smile before turning back to Maddi and lowering my voice. We're not in school, they can't reprimand me for the topic or words, but that doesn't stop the extremely uncomfortable stares. "All I'm saying is we can at least give it a shot. Otherwise, we sit here and accept the fact that Abi might not come home. Do you want that?"

"No," she says.

"Me either."

"You seem so... cavalier about all of this."

It's the stress of the situation.

I draw in a deep breath and exhale slowly. She's right. I'm not showing much emotion on the subject. "I'll let you in on a little secret. I'm just as freaked out as you, but I learned a long time ago that giving in to the emotions clouds your thinking." I pull in the corners of my lips and raise my eyebrows before sitting back. "You want to get things done? You keep a clear head and make a plan. So... let's do that."

"You make it sound so easy."

"It's not. I've had lots of practice." I shrug. "Let's start with you telling me what happened that night."

FIVE

Days since Abi's disappearance: 8

She draws in a slow, tentative breath, and I can tell this is going to be *some kind* of story. "Okay, so—"

Oh boy. Here we go.

"—Abi came home from the library, Dad had finished making dinner, everything was normal... kind of. After he got home from work, he grabbed the mail and found *the* envelope. You know, the big manila ones that the acceptance letters come in because they have all the New Student Orientation information and whatever." She waves a hand in front of her face.

People always look so weird when they do that.

"One moment the house was its usual, quiet self, and the next she was squealing. She ran into my room and showed me the letter, but, like, a second later Dad was calling her downstairs. I couldn't catch a lot of it, but there was shouting. From what I could hear, Dad was going on about how she applied to BCC behind his back — blah, blah, blah. You've seen how Dad gets. He's vile when he's mad, and he says a bunch of nasty things he wouldn't normally say. He was angry, screaming..." her words trail off, and I can see a visible change in her demeanor. She's a smaller version of herself now, more timid. I've seen Abi do the same thing after those big fights. I hate that he affects them like this.

"Hey," I duck my head to try to catch her gaze and give an encouraging smile. If I can keep her talking, I can keep her in this stable place and the tears at bay. "So, they fought... what happened next?"

"Uhm..." She takes another drink from the mug. "I was still upstairs, so I don't know what happened definitively, but there was a crash. I think something was thrown? All I know is I saw Dad cleaning up broken glass when I came down. Either way, whatever happened was enough to make Abi say 'that's enough' and leave. She walked out without, well, anything, really. I don't think she even had shoes on. She was just... gone."

"Yeah, that sounds like Abs." I sniff and silence settles between us again. A *hmm* vibrates at the base of my throat while mulling all the information over. "Was she seen with anyone?"

Maddi does that thing where she retreats into her thoughts while looking out the window and taking a drink again. "I don't—Oh!" She looks at me with wide, bright eyes. A glimmer of hope.

"I did overhear the cops telling Dad about this white car someone saw her get into a street or two over from the house. When the paper ran the article about Abi being missing, some guy called the station about it. I guess he was night gardening when he saw her walking down the road? Who night gardens? What even *is* night gardening?"

Presumably when you garden... at night.

"Anyway, from what I heard, the guy said he remembered because she was crying and doing her angry mumble — you know, the one where she has those little fights with herself where she says all the things she *wanted* to say but didn't think of in the moment? Well, when the cops came over for a follow-up interview, they saw our white car in the driveway and asked if either of us picked her up that night, but neither of us left the house." She pauses. I can almost see the events of the night play behind her eyes like a movie. She's fixating, going over every detail of the night and following conversations with the cops that she's mentally logged. "I should've gone after her. I'm stupid for not doing that."

"You're not stupid. There's no way you could've known that something like this would happen." I'm trying to say the right thing. Guilt is common in situations like this, isn't it? Especially when you're close with the person. It's no secret to anyone that Abi and Maddi are almost as close as Em and me. With only being a year apart, the two are as thick as thieves as much as they're at each other's throats. At the end of the day, though, the love they share with each other is one that overrides any conflict they have.

"Thanks for saying that."

I nod.

With a deep breath in, Maddi releases it quickly in that way most people do when they're trying to shake an emotion away. "Anyway, I ended up texting her a little while after she left." She pulls her purse off her lap and sets it on the table to grab her phone. I watch her click through a few screens and turn it toward me. "See? This was probably — what? — thirty minutes after she left? I asked if she was okay, and she said she's getting milkshakes with 'him,' and... that was it."

"Him?" I stare at the texts as my left eyebrow rises.

MADELEINE: HEY, YOU OKAY?

ABIGAIL: YEAH, FINE. GETTING MILKSHAKES WITH HIM. BE HOME WHENEVER.

MADELEINE: OKAY, BE SAFE.

MADELEINE: I DIDN'T HEAR YOU GET UP THIS MORNING, DID YOU LEAVE EARLY?

MADELEINE: ABS... YOU OKAY?

MADELEINE: ABI, PLEASE. ANSWER THE PHONE.

Maddi's worry is practically audible in the texts.

I look up from the phone and adjust myself to sit a little higher in the chair. "Who is this *him* supposed to be?"

"I assumed it was you," she says.

"Nope." I shake my head. "Wait. Did you tell the cops about this?"

"No. I was worried it would turn back on you. The first person they always look at is either the parent or the significant other. We both know you wouldn't do anything to hurt her." Maddi takes a moment to exhale a sigh, then tilts her head back down toward her cup. "Besides, who does she spend time with besides us? It makes sense to assume it was you."

She has a point.

"Thanks for that, I guess." Based on the grimace she gives me, my tone probably sounds sarcastic. "I mean it, Maddi. *Thank you.*" I rub the back of my neck. I wish Em were here; she'd know what to do next. She's always better at this stuff. "You said the cops ruled out your dad?"

Offense takes over her expression. "I was there all night with him. After Abi left, we had dinner, watched a movie, and I went upstairs to study before going to sleep."

I try to recall what I'd learned from those cop shows Em always puts on. I can't stand noise when I'm reading, but she just has to have it. She says it's something about a ringing in her ears or how the silence is loud. I don't get it, but every once in a while when I get sick of trying to block the noise out, I end up watching whatever it is she's left on. I'm convinced that's how she gets around my refusal to watch mystery movies with her. "Has anyone searched her room?"

"For what?" she asks.

"*Anything.* Don't you girls keep diaries or something? Write down your every move throughout the day or what makes you upset or something?"

Maddi means to scoff — I can see the annoyance in her eyes — but it comes out as a laugh. It's the first time I've seen anything more than a fake smile from her in days. "You're such a boy, Hunter Greene. Ugh. Yeah, I think she keeps a journal, but I don't know where it is."

"Have you looked?"

"No. I'm not going to invade her privacy like that."

"Well, Madeleine Perkins—"

I can use your full name too.

"—you have a choice to make." My voice takes on a more theatrical tone. It's not that I'm trying to make light of the situation, I want to try to find Abi as quickly as possible, but my plan of distracting her has worked so far. I might as well keep going. "Either you invade her privacy to try to figure out who *him* is, or you *don't* invade her privacy and forever wonder if you could've solved the mystery of what happened to your sister."

She scrunches her nose. "Don't do that."

"Do what?" My smile is wide, toothy, innocent. I know exactly what she's talking about, but it's fun to poke the bear sometimes.

"Make finding my sister sound like some detective game."

"Isn't it though? And who doesn't like solving a good mystery?"

Okay, there's the cavalier nature, but humor is how I cope.

"Seriously, though, I'm doing this with or without you."

Her face scrunches and contorts as she contemplates both options. Where Abi is an impulsive, caution-to-the-wind kind of person, Maddi is all about calculations and making sure whatever she does is the right thing before she actually does it. "I couldn't forgive myself if we didn't at least try," she says finally.

"Atta girl!" My hand slaps the table, causing a small pause in the noise of the café. "Tomorrow?"

She shakes her head. "Dad will be home, but he works late Friday. Come over after school and we can look through things."

"That works. Em's going to Cai's lacrosse game that night, so I'll be flying solo again."

"A rare occurrence."

"Yeah, yeah." I say and roll my eyes.

"He's still making time for sports with all the college classes?"

I shrug half-heartedly. "It's his last year of traditional schooling. He's dropping out to start the fire fighter training next fall."

She nods. I can tell she's mulling something over, but I can't place my finger on what. "Well, hopefully she has fun." Maddi forces a smile. Whatever she's thinking about, it's not pleasant. "Surprised you're not going."

I study her for a moment then draw in a deep breath. "I don't because the whole thing bores me — not that Em likes it either, but... she has to support the boyfriend, right?"

Maddi hesitates and looks down at her mug again. "Right."

Six

Days since Abi's disappearance: 12

The following days were a complete blur. Once it gets out that the cops aren't trying to find Abi anymore, people start reaching out. They asked if I was okay, if I needed anything, if I'd been talking to Maddi and her dad about things, if anyone has heard from Abi... I had no answers for them. Hell, I *still* have no answers, and it's becoming harder and harder to not drown in the emotions I've told Maddi she should try to ignore. Everyone else might think it's stupid or that we're too young to know what love is, but this girl? I'd give up anything for her.

In the haze of everything, I manage to find time to ask around and discover where Abi was last seen — Boltz Street — and who the guy is that was *night gardening*. His name is Samuel Jenkins. He's an older gentleman who volunteers at the community center and once tried to run for head of the PTA despite having no children at the school anymore. He says it's because he has good ideas and wants to make a difference in the school system. When he didn't win, the school offered for him to be a volunteer football coach instead.

"Can I help you?" he asks after my third knock.

"Hi, Mr. Jenkins?" I put on my most charming smile.

He studies me trying to figure out whether I'm here for a real reason or I'm casing the house. It wouldn't be the first time someone was so bold. "Depends on the party asking." He steps onto the porch and closes the door behind him.

I step back to give him space. "My name's Hunter Greene. Abigail Perkins, the girl that's missing, she's my girlfriend."

"Oh, I'm so sorry, kid." Sadness replaces the pity I've heard so often lately. It's refreshing, and at least I know there's real concern. "I lost my wife eight years ago, and I can only imagine what you must be going through." He gestures to a bench under the front window. "Here, let's sit down."

Once we're settled, everything starts to hit at once; the idea that Abi might really be gone, that someone could've taken her, that she might be hurt. Or worse. Breathing is hard. My chest is tight, and my lungs burn. Panic. Anxiety.

Am I breathing? When did I start holding my breath? Breathe. I need to breathe.

I do my best to ignore all of it and force myself to turn toward him. "I-I was wondering if you could tell me about that night. I thought I could try to find something the cops missed. They think that she ran away, but that's not her. That's not—" I stop myself, I'm rambling. "I'm sorry."

"Hey." He must see through the attempts to hide my emotions because his words grow soft and fatherly. "Kid, you're going through something traumatic. Don't apologize."

After a moment of silence, he takes in a deep breath, rubs his palms on the tops of his jeans, and stares forward. Just like with Maddi, I can see the events being played behind his eyes. "It was probably... half past nine? Maybe it was ten come to think of it. I work most of the day, and when I come home, I like to relax, have dinner, and then watch a program or two, but on Tuesdays and Thursdays, I garden." He waits to see if I'm going to say something, and when I don't, he continues. "It was something my wife and I did when she was still alive."

I smile.

That's sweet.

"When I saw her, she was walking down the sidewalk mumbling to herself. I remember because I thought it was odd that a young girl would be walking down the road so late by herself. I asked if she was okay, and when she looked over, her face was puffy like she'd been crying. She nodded, thanked me for asking, and continued walking. Not even a minute later, a car showed up. The driver rolled down the passenger window and said something to her. I assume it was an invitation to get in the car, because at first she refused and tried to keep walking, but whatever the person said next convinced her to get in."

Abi, no. Who was that? What did they say to you? Why did you get in the car?

"Did you see the driver? Did you hear what they said?"

Mr. Jenkins shakes his head. "No, I'm sorry. They were too far away for me to pick up on anything, and with how dark it was, the inside of the car was all shadows."

I sigh, and based on the glance Mr. Jenkins gives me, he's sorry that he can't give me more information. A look of pity replaces sadness making him look like every other person in my life right now.

It's okay, it's not your fault.

"I know it was a white car, but is there anything else you can tell me about it? License plate? Bumper stickers? Anything?" I ask.

We sit in silence as he gives my questions some thought — his eyes squint, and he presses his lips into a thin line. "I didn't see a license plate. I don't remember any bumper stickers, but... you know... the passenger window had this horrible squeak to it when it rolled down."

Hey, it's something.

After mulling over everything he'd told me, I force a smile. "Well, I don't want to take up any more of your time."

"I'm sorry I don't have more information to give you, but I hope you find her, and I hope she's safe."

"Me too."

SEVEN

Days since Abi's disappearance: 12

It's nearly dark by the time I make it to the Perkinses house. At the café, Maddi said her father was staying late at work, but how late is *late*? Do we still have enough time to search Abi's room?

"There you are!" She grabs me by the front of my shirt and pulls me into the house. Instincts from living with Em kick in, and I swat her hand away a little more forcefully than I intend to. There's the loud slapping sound of skin on skin, and I immediately offer an uncomfortable, apologetic smile.

"Sorry. Habit. Em and I—"

"Yeah, yeah. I know, I've seen you two wrestle." Her tone is flat and almost annoyed, but she waves it off and continues walking further into the house. "Dad shouldn't be home for a couple of hours, so we have time before you need to rush out," she says.

"Rush out?" I take off my jacket, drop it over my backpack by the door, and jog after her.

The Perkinses' home is set up like every other cookie-cutter house in our neighborhood: two stories, small living and dining rooms, and anywhere from one to three bedrooms depending on the family size. The Perkinses' home is a modest, simple three-bedroom with a trophy fish collection worthy of a bachelor pad.

"C'mon, Hunter, you really think it's a good idea for you to be caught here?" she asks. "Dad's still pissed."

"Makes sense." It doesn't, and my tone reflects that, but Maddi doesn't say anything in response.

There was a time I was welcomed like part of the family. I didn't have to knock, was able to stay as long as I wanted, and pick up Abi whenever. Now, I'm ostracized. All of that hard work I'd done to be accepted by her family has been washed down the drain by one decision her father doesn't like because it isn't in line with "their plan." Now, because of a fight pertaining to that decision, Abi is missing and he's convinced himself it's my fault.

If anyone should be to blame, it's you. You caused this. You made her leave because you couldn't let her make her own decisions. You couldn't just let her be happy. For once.

I let Maddi go up the stairs first so I can take a few deep breaths. The more the thoughts rage, the angrier I get.

At least he's not a cop. At least he's not one of the people who were supposed to be looking for her.

Once we're upstairs, Maddi doesn't hesitate to go into Abi's room, but I pause in the doorway. It feels wrong to be here without Abi. My mind plays little snippets of a memory: her laughing while pulling me into the room through the window, me shushing her, her pulling me into a kiss that causes fireworks behind my eyes.

It's not the same without you here.

The room breathes Abi and completely contrasts the rest of the house. It's a flurry of different colors with no theme, cork boards with pictures and paint swatches and old drawings tacked onto them, shoes and random pieces of clothing scattered around the floor that she always says she'll pick up later. People always say artists are known for having messy rooms. It used to bother me how she doesn't care about living in a mess, but now I'm craving the promises we both know she never keeps.

The last time I'd been in here, we were sitting on the bed together. I can still see the scene so clearly. My back is leaning against the wall with her back against my chest, my arms are around her with that teal blanket she loves so much over our legs. She's reading a book we'd been assigned in English. Her voice is always so calming when she reads. I constantly tell her she's meant to tell stories.

"Hunter?" Maddi's voice pulls me out of my thoughts like the shock of an ice bath.

I take a quick breath in and look at her. "Yeah, what's up?"

"You okay? We don't have to do this today if it's too much."

"Ye-yeah. No, I'm fine. Sorry." After clearing my throat, I move to Abi's bookshelf. It's filled with different how-to-draw books and the classics everyone says they love but have never read. Abi's read every single one.

"I'm sorry that you're having to deal with all this," she says. She's trying to make conversation. Maddi hates silence, it makes her uncomfortable, and she hates tension filled silence even more. Trust me, there's a lot of tension being back here.

I don't say anything and keep scanning the bookshelf.

"Did you ever go talk to that guy that saw the car?" The push and pull of metal tracks tells me she's going through the drawers of the dresser.

That's a strange place to start, but maybe you know something I don't.

"Yeah," I say and launch into the details of the conversation with Mr. Jenkins. When she doesn't respond, I glance in her direction. It looks like she's staring at something on the dresser, but the longer I study her, the more obvious it becomes that she's looking passed whatever it is in front of her.

She's processing.

EIGHT

Days since Abi's disappearance: 12

Once satisfied with my overview of the bookshelf, I move to the desk. Much like the rest of her room, the desk is an assortment of colors and items strewn about. Abi's laptop still sits front and center, accompanied by a cup holding different paint brushes with another next to it jam-packed with pens and pencils and highlighters all in varying stages of disarray.

My chaotic, messy girl.

After taking a seat in the desk chair, I open the laptop, and the loading screen brings everything to life. There's a scenic photo of a mountain range that's half-covered with different folders and icons. As I read the folder's labels and contents, the idea of Abi being completely disorganized is put to the test. There's a folder for each school year, and inside of that is a folder for each semester, inside of that is a folder for each class, and inside of *that* is a document for every paper or essay she'd completed.

This is the most organized thing I've ever seen from you, Abi.

I'm trying to look for anything out of the ordinary, but continuously come up short.

"This is just school stuff," I say and continue clicking through folders.

"Yeah, Abi didn't use that thing unless it was necessary." Maddi pauses. "Try her search history."

Good idea.

I pull up the browser history and scan through it. Abi doesn't use technology often. She's always going on about how society is too dependent on electronics and how she only keeps a phone because it allows her to instantly connect with her favorite people. Because of that, there are week-long gaps in the browser history, but the ones from the last month immediately pop out.

"Hey, Mads." My eyes are glued to the screen.

"Hunter Greene, did you call me *Mads?*" she asks, disgusted.

"S-sorry—hey, did Abi ever mention someone following her?" The collision of her hand against the back of my head causes a *thwap* sound and a sting. "Ow! What the hell?" My head ducks forward while a hand reaches back to rub where she'd hit me.

"*Don't* call me Mads." The Perkins girls have a tone they use when they want someone to know they're serious. Abi never uses it on me, but I've seen her use it on people at school. It's scary. "My mom called me that. Don't *ever* call me Mads."

"My bad, jeez."

She glares at me for a moment, then nods toward the computer. "What'd you find?"

I highlight a few of the searches listed before reading them to her. "*How to know if someone's following you. What are the signs of a stalker? Psychology behind obsession.* She didn't mention any of this to you?" It's hard to keep the worry from my tone. This is proof Abi has a stalker, right? This is proof that something might've been going on?

Someone could've been following her, someone could've taken her.

She shakes her head, but never turns away from the screen. "No. Nothing." Those gears are turning again, and I assume she must be going over every interaction she's had with Abi in the last couple of weeks. "She had mentioned this kid from her science class — what's his name — dang it. It's her lab partner."

"Jasper." I push the chair away from the desk and swivel it to face her, forcing her to step back.

"Yeah! Him. She said he's quiet and a little... *odd*. I guess he follows her around sometimes. I don't think he has many friends," she says, then leans against the desk and crosses her arms.

"Okay, well, let's keep looking for now. We can come back to that later."

Note to self: grab a notebook to write everything down. It's time to start keeping track of things.

I close the laptop and continue searching through the things on the desk while Maddi starts checking the bedside table and under the bed. I try to remind myself not to jump too far, too fast and move on from the idea that someone is stalking Abi, but it's hard to. When we set out with this plan, I prepared myself to find something, but I never prepared myself for this. Why hasn't she told me? The whole thing makes the knot in my stomach twist further.

Don't get ahead of yourself, Hunter. Right now, it's just search history. There's nothing backing up that someone was actually following her. She wants to be a writer, remember? Maybe it's for a story.

But is it?

"Bingo!" The sound is triumphant. When I turn to glance at her, she's holding up a journal with a ton of tiny flowers all over the cover. She sits on the bed and begins thumbing through it.

"Do you th—" my words are cut off by the front door opening and a bellowing voice.

"I'm home!"

Mr. Perkins.

My heart starts to race.

We hear you're home, but the real question is why?

Maddi jumps to her feet, abandoning the journal on the bed. What's on her face now is terror. "Hi, Daddy," she calls out.

There's a shift in the house. The silence that lingers after Maddi's reply is too long, too quiet. It's electrified like the air before a heavy storm. "Madeleine Perkins!"

He's mad. No, not mad. Furious.

"I thought you said a couple hours," I say, trying to keep my voice at a whisper.

"It was supposed to be!" She tries to match my tone, but panic is already setting in.

Great. How am I supposed to get out of this?

"You answer me right *now*, young lady! Whose things are by this door!?"

My heart hammers faster against my chest.

I left my jacket and backpack downstairs.

I give her an apologetic smile. I should've brought them upstairs with us, but I thought we had more time.

Yikes. My fault.

"No one's!" She shoos me toward the bathroom.

Once I'm passed the threshold, she scurries out of Abi's room and closes the door behind her. Everything sounds dull and muffled now, but one wonderful thing about these one-size-fits-all homes is that the walls are super thin making eavesdropping easy. The walls shake as Mr. Perkins stomps up the stairs. The closer he gets, the shallower my breathing becomes. Adrenaline is coursing through me like a bullet train at full speed. What if he finds me? He's already mad. Will he yell at me? I can handle that, but I don't want Maddi to take the heat.

"You want to try that answer again?" It sounds like he's right outside Abi's door, and it's obvious he knows she's lying. Of course, he knows. He's seen my stuff a thousand times. "Where's Hunter?"

There it is.

"Hunter! Get out here!"

Nope. Not a chance.

He calls for me again, but I stay put.

"Daddy, no one's here." She sighs, and the heaviness behind it tells me she's trying to convince him of whatever is about to be said. "I didn't want you to be mad, okay? I'm sorry. I probably shouldn't have brought them in the house, but I didn't want to just leave them either. I stayed after school to study at the library. Hunter was there and asked me to watch his things for a second while he went to go find a book, but he didn't come back — before you ask, I don't know why — so I figured I'd just return them tomorrow or something. I'd leave them on the porch at their house and go. No contact, like I promised. It was a stupid idea, I'm sorry." There's a pause before Maddi continues. "Do you want some tea?" There's the faint sound of someone sighing heavily, but I can't tell who it comes from. "Come, I'll make us some tea."

A muffled sound comes as a response to her words, and while I'm not sure what is said, the footsteps fading away tells me he must've agreed. Once I'm sure they're downstairs, I sneak out of the bathroom and look around to find Abi's laptop and journal. We have two potential pieces of evidence. That constitutes a successful search, right? Sure, we haven't had a chance to look through each item thoroughly, but it's better than nothing.

Me: Taking the laptop for more research. Will keep it safe and get it back soon. You search the journal.
Madeleine: Got it. I'll leave your things on the porch and tell you when it's safe to grab them.

The backside of the Perkinses' house has a rose ladder with creeping ivy that interlaces with the flowers. It's beautiful in the summer, but it's not easy to climb when everything is in full bloom. I'm not sure how many times I've made the climb up and down from this window over the last three years, but I've never done it with my arms half full.

This is going to be fun.

After gathering the charging cord and laptop, I open Abi's window as quietly as possible and drop the cord to the ground. One less thing to carry means one less thing to worry about. On a normal fall evening, this climb down is a breeze — the ivy is scarce, the flowers are out of season — but with a laptop in one arm, it's a challenge. I almost drop the damn thing twice on the way down, but once on the ground, I collect the cord and check my phone.

MADELEINE: STUFF'S OUTSIDE. PULLING DAD INTO THE LIVING ROOM. MOVE QUICK!

There's no hesitation. I shove my phone back in my pocket, crouch to a hunched position, and jog around to the front of the house before throwing the items in my backpack and bolting.

I run two blocks before stopping. I'm out of breath, my heart's still pounding, but at least I get out of there unnoticed. Mostly. After collapsing onto the sidewalk, I stare at the sky and try to bring my breathing back to normal. My mind reels with everything I know now. Mr. Jenkins saw Abi and gave a description of the car, there's search history suggesting someone is stalking her. When I'm finally able to stop gasping for air, I pull my phone back out and sit up.

ME: THANK YOU. SORRY ABOUT THE TROUBLE. KEEP ME UPDATED ABOUT THE JOURNAL.
MADELEINE: DON'T WORRY ABOUT IT AND WILL DO.

Nine

Days since Abi's disappearance: 12

I'm not even halfway through the door when Mom comes around the corner from the kitchen. The telltale signs of her bustling around the kitchen are present: hair in a messy bun with small, frizzy pieces framing her face, a wrinkled apron splotched with food and grease stains, and rosy cheeks. Some of my favorite memories with Mom are her like this. Because I was the hyperactive one between us when we were younger, I used to help Mom clean on Saturdays while Em read.

"Where have you been?" Between the question and her appearance, an onlooker would assume she's frantic.

"I know, I know, I'm sorry. I went to visit Maddi, and I lost track of time and her dad came home an—"

She cuts me off and says, "I'm just glad you're safe." The smile she gives me before heading back into the kitchen softens the meaning behind her words. She's a blunt woman, and it often gets misconstrued by people around us as her being rude or abrasive. I've been told by many people Mom worries too much and she's too over protective, but what they don't understand is how much she's been through. She never used to be so overbearing. Strict, yes, but the constant need to know where we are is more recent.

Two years ago, we lost Dad to a car accident. He was a salesman at one of the furniture places downtown and stayed late one night to finish inventory paperwork. While on his drive home, someone ran through an intersection and hit the driver's side of Dad's car. The cops said his death was instantaneous, but part of me believes they told Mom that out of a desire to comfort her.

I remember staying up with Mom when Dad didn't come home. She yelled at me to go to bed, but something didn't feel right. You know how people always say you can *feel* when something's happened to the people you love? That you might not know how to describe it, but you'll have an urge to reach out and make sure they're okay? I felt it that night, and I'm pretty sure Mom did too. I watched her from the living room couch as she paced through the kitchen, dining room, living room, then back again, calling him over and over. He was never late, and if he was, he made sure to check in.

"He always answers. Something's wrong," I remember her telling me. I'll never forget the worry I saw in her that night. When the cops finally came to the house to deliver the news, she crumbled right in the doorway. I held Mom and Em the rest of the night after that. I was the strong one then, just like I need to be the strong one now.

It was a hard time in the Greene household for a while after that. For the first few days, Mom barely left her bed. When she did, it was to lay on the couch or because Em and I were forcing her to come downstairs to eat something. She was lost to the depths of her sorrow more than she was present. Once she finally started functioning again, she barely let us out of her sight — she wouldn't even let us go to school the first week. She claimed it was because we needed time to grieve, but Em and I knew it was really because she needed someone there and was probably terrified that something would happen to us too. Our privilege to leave the house was eventually given back, but only after we promised to abide by a "text me where you're going, who you're with, and when you get there" rule. If we didn't do it or forgot, she'd call every two minutes until we answered. She's better about it now, but she still hovers and worries.

I drop my shoes by the door and set my backpack on the couch before following her into the kitchen. "Is Em home?"

"She should be soon," she says while stirring something on the stove.

"Gotcha. Well, will you tell her I wanna talk to her when she gets here?"

"Of course, *mijo*." Her words are accompanied by her turning from the pot and cupping my cheek. "Is everything okay?"

I nod. "*Sí, mama.* Don't worry, it's just class stuff."

No, it's not, and I'm sorry I'm lying to you.

"I've got homework to do, so I'm gonna head upstairs and do that, okay?" The faster I can get away from her, the less chance I have of getting caught. Mom is good at calling my bluff. Always has been.

"Are you hungry? Dinner will be done soon."

"Nah, not right now, but save me a plate?" I kiss her cheek then make my way back into the living room to grab my backpack and head upstairs.

After pulling out the laptop and setting it on the bed, I grab a notebook from my desk. With so much being discovered, it's important to make a list of all the evidence we find and any suspects we may have. We can't afford to gather an important clue and forget it or lose it all because we don't write it down. But where to start? I take a seat on my bed, open to a blank page, and stare at the blue lines.

Evidence:

Laptop. Search history: was searching for information about stalkers.

Journal. TBD.

Car. Possibly white or tan, passenger side window squeaks when being rolled down.

Suspect List:

Jasper. Abi's science partner. Follows her around.

Michael Perkins. Abi's dad. Owns a white car, frustrated/angry with her for applying to BCC.

I hesitate and hover over Mr. Perkins' name, wondering if I should scratch it out. Part of me feels like having his name on the list doesn't feel right. He's her dad. He's supposed to love her, but with a temper like his...

Is it possible? I've never seen him lay a hand on them before.

But who's to say things didn't change, and usually the victim knows the perpetrator, right? That's what all the shows and movies say; start with the people closest to the victim and work outward.

"Whatcha doooin'?" Em's voice is playful, and I can hear the smirk even before I look up.

"Writing out information about Abi."

For Abi? This isn't for Abi. Technically, it's for me and my search to prove she was taken.

"So, you're really doing this, huh?" She flops onto her stomach on the bed with her chin resting in her palms. "Trying to find her?"

"I owe it to her."

We stare at each other for a few moments before Em sighs and looks toward my comforter. There's worry behind that sound. "It's not going to bring him back, you know."

I hate that she's always in my head, I hate it even more when she's there before me. She doesn't need to tell me who *him* is, and I don't need to question who she's talking about either.

Dad... But that's not what this is. I know what you're thinking. I'm not projecting.

There's a softer side to Em that not many people see. One she saves for people closest to her. When it comes out, she's gentle and sympathetic, but she can play therapist and psychologist in those moments too. On more than one occasion, Em has told me I'm taking whatever unresolved trauma I have toward losing our dad and projecting it onto things in my current life, but that's not what this is. I'm trying to find Abi. I'm trying to bring her home. I'm trying to make sure she's safe.

Then why is there guilt? Why is there a little part that feels saving Abi will help?

"I know," I say. It's a lie.

"Look," she sits up to cross her legs. "I miss Dad too, and I miss Abi, but don't drive yourself crazy with this, okay?"

"I need to find her. The cops gave up on her and..." My words trail off. The idea of going through any type of loss like what happened with Dad hits me all at once. Maybe I am projecting. Maybe I am using Abi as a way to make up for not saving Dad somehow, but is that wrong? It's also a motivator too, right? If I'm passionate about saving her, I'll keep fighting and not give up. I try to swallow, but my spit gets stuck in my throat until I force it down.

"Are you going to help or not?"

"Does a cow moo? C'mon, now," she says as she nudges me with her foot.

I push her foot away with a gagging noise, earning a laugh from her so loud it echoes off my walls. Laughter, that's something this house hasn't heard in a while. It's nice. It's comforting.

"Whatcha got? Show me." She waves me over to her and moves so I can sit next to her. After opening Abi's laptop to show her the search history, I start explaining the events of the day.

"So, there's not much to go on yet," Em says after a moment of silence.

"Well, no, but it's only the first day. I'd say it's off to a decent start though. We found proof that she might've had someone following her or a stalker. That's *something*, right?"

Em raises her right shoulder to her ear for a half-shrug. "Sure, I guess." She doesn't want me getting ahead of myself, and I understand but... "Let's see if Maddi finds anything in the journal."

TEN

Days since Abi's disappearance: 13

The buzzing of my phone causes a sleep-infused groan. My hand blindly slaps at the nightstand, but when I don't find it right away, I lift my head and find myself in a sea of old test papers and homework assignments. I'm not sure when I fell asleep, but by the time I did, every inch of the laptop had been looked through. Everything from apps to browsers to photos to chats... but there is nothing other than the troubling search history. It wasn't until Em noticed we were three hours into our little information finding excursion that she convinced me to put the brain power toward studying for finals. They are still several weeks away, but studying over time means no last-minute cramming.

MADELEINE: YOU UP?

MADELEINE: NEED TO TALK TO YOU.

MADELEINE: COMING OVER. FOUND INFO.

ME: SORRY, JUST WOKE UP. GIVE ME 20.

MADELEINE: EM AROUND? DOES SHE KNOW YET?

ME: PROBABLY, AND YEAH. TOLD HER ABOUT IT LAST NIGHT.

MADELEINE: OKAY. BE THERE IN 20.

After putting the laptop and notebook under my bed, I poke my head into the hallway.

"Em! You up? Maddi's coming over."

"Yeah! Got coffee waiting for you."

Man, you're the best.

"OhmygodIhavesomuchtotellyou," Maddi says in a high-pitched, rapid-fire way that jumbles her words together.

Em blinks a couple of times, obviously trying to figure out what Maddi said, and I pull my mug to my lips for a sip of coffee to hide my smile.

"I'm sorry, what was that language?" Em asks.

"Be nice." A head nod signals them to follow me upstairs.

Maddi pauses at my door and looks around. "Your room is so... clean."

"Hunter's the OCD one out of us," Em says as she sits on the floor and crosses her legs. "Always has to have things in place. *Pristine.*" She slides her hands across the space in front of her as if reading a billboard. "I don't understand it. Life should contain a little chaos, but... I guess that's why he has me." She beams a proud smile.

You're so stupid.

"Anywaaay," I draw out the word a little longer than it needs to be. "We're getting off task. Have a seat anywhere." It's not until the offer is made that I realize I never picked up the compilation of items on the bed. After setting my mug on the nightstand, I scoop the papers up into a smaller pile so there's room for both of us.

"What are those?" Maddi asks.

"Studying material. Finals are coming up," I say.

She gives me a look that reads *you've got to be kidding me,* then looks back at the bed with hesitation.

"Don't worry, those papers are probably the dirtiest thing on that bed," Em says.

Oh, here we go again. You're a menace.

"He changes his sheets no less than twice a week." Em cups her mouth with one hand as if trying to cover her mouth from me, but the words are said at a normal volume.

After sitting down on the bed and throwing a pillow at her, a squinty-eyed sneer is shot her way while she writhes in laughter. "You know *other* people are supposed to laugh at your jokes, right?"

"Excuse you! I'm hilarious." Em scoffs in fake offense and lays back on the ground with the pillow under her head, feet propped up on the bed. "You're lucky to have me as the comedic relief in your life, Hunter Mateo."

I shift on the bed so my back's against the wall, legs stretched out in front of me, while Maddi perches herself at the foot of the bed. "I'll try to remember that, Emerald Alexis."

Em makes a face, and I beam a mirror of her earlier smile.

"You two done?" Maddi asks.

Em and I nod.

"I stayed up all night trying to find *something*. There was this weird little bookmark — well, I assumed it was a bookmark — near the last few entries. When I pulled it out, it was just a strip of paper."

She hands me a ripped piece of stationery with little ravens scattered in the margins. Most are in different stages of flight, but in the two corners not ripped off, there's an armchair with a bird sitting and staring to the side. In the middle of the paper, scrawled in scratchy handwriting are the words *Din U&M 8.*

I look at Maddi, then back at the paper. "What does it mean?"

Maddi shrugs.

"Think it has something to do with all this?" I ask.

"No clue, dude," she says.

"What does it say?" Em turns her head toward me but makes no effort to get up.

I read, "Din U-and-M eight."

Em stares at the ceiling for a few moments, shrugs, and says, "No idea...."

"Okay, well, for now let's table whatever this is." I set the piece of stationery on the bed and lean toward Maddi to try to read the journal over her shoulder.

"Most of the journal is filled with the stuff I expected to find: Hunter this, Hunter that. Em, Cai, Hunter, and I went on this date, and it was cute. I failed a test, yada yada." She flips through a bunch of pages and stops at one of the later entries. "But this one—" She hands me the journal. "—Caught my eye."

I stare at the looped words filling the page. More flashes of memories flood my mind — passing notes in class, leaving cute messages in each other's notebooks — all things I'm very worried I'll never do or get again. I force myself to take a deep breath and read the passage in front of me out loud.

"D is getting more and more upset when I tell him I can't make or keep plans. Three days ago, I had to tell him I couldn't meet him at the diner because I had a date with Hunter, and he got so angry. He started texting me over and over about how he could make me happier than Hunter could, how I deserved a better life than what I'll get with him. He's done this before. It's uncomfortable, not to mention it hurts to hear those things."

I pause.

"You okay?" Em asks.

I nod and continue.

"When I didn't respond, he changed his tune and started apologizing. I'm not sure what to do. Do you think it's possible he's not all there? You know, in the head? Is this what having a stalker is? I don't want to worry anyone. I'll do research on my own first."

"He sounds like a creep," Em says. "Who is *D* anyway?" She lifts her head and glances between Maddi and me.

Maddi shrugs. "Doesn't say, but the entry is from about a month ago. It lines up with the search history from her laptop." She takes the journal and flips through several more pages. "Later on, she says it felt like he was getting too close, and she was starting to contemplate telling someone."

"Well, it's obvious that this *D* person is the reason she was researching stalkers." I extend my hand in a silent request for the journal and Maddi hands it back to me. "The first passage mentioned a diner. You think that's the *him* she met for milkshakes?"

Maddi's face scrunches. "It's possible."

"What are you two talking about?" Em asks.

"When Maddi and I met at the café, she showed me a text from Abi saying she's getting milkshakes with someone. She only referred to him as *him*."

"I assumed it was Hunter, but—"

"He was home with me," Em says.

"Exactly," I say.

ELEVEN

Days since Abi's disappearance: 13

There's a silence that engulfs the room as we all think about everything we've found and discussed.

So, Abi has a stalker — or at least someone that is getting possessive of her — and it's likely that someone is who met up with her the day she disappeared.

"Yesterday, Maddi mentioned Jasper, Abi's science partner," I say.

"You think he's involved in this?" Em asks.

I shrug.

"Well — hmm — I don't know the details, but there was this one time Abi told me he left a note in her locker saying how he was thankful someone was finally nice to him and how he thought she was one of the prettiest girls in school or something." Em drops her head back on the pillow to stare at the ceiling. "Is it really possible he could've done this? The dude seems pretty spineless."

"Has anyone seen him in school since Abi disappeared?" Maddi asks.

"I don't pay attention to the kid," I say.

"I can keep an eye out for him," Em says. "Pretty sure he drives a white car — wait, maybe it's tan."

"Why do you even know that?" I ask.

Bro, that's grounds for being a stalker. I just got you to stop breaking into abandoned houses, don't tell me you've taken to wandering around town watching people's lives.

"Hello! C'mon, Hunter! You need to pay attention to these things. You can't tell me you're surprised that I keep track of small details with all the crime shows I watch. They always talk about how it's the smallest details that crack the case. Keep track of the small things, and the big things fit themselves together like puzzle pieces." She sits up. "I know Becky Wizchoski was given her mom's beat up Chrysler, even though she says she's just borrowing it from her, and Dalton Matthews *says* that motorcycle is his, but it's really his dad's."

The thought of Em having a list of what everyone drives and what they do in their spare time is unsettling. I've never thought about paying attention to that stuff. After all, why would it matter in a normal setting? "You're watching too much TV, dude," I say.

"She'd be a good detective," Maddi says.

"Nah. I use my powers for the good of myself and those I love. I don't need the law trying to dictate where my efforts go." Em gives that proud smile again.

"You're a little scary sometimes."

Em lets out a high-pitched giggle and says, "Thank you! You're so kind."

"Okay, you two. About Jasper, there's at least — what do they call it, Em? Reasonable suspicion?"

"I *knew* you paid attention to those shows. You like them, Hunter, admit it. *Admit it!*" She throws the pillow at me.

I hold my arms up to block the incoming object and laugh. "You're out of your mind. I hate those things."

She rolls her eyes. "So, what's the plan, Stan?"

"If we can find it, I'd say the diner is the next step. There's a chance someone will remember them," I say.

"So, there's a diner she describes in here." Maddi picks up the journal, turns to an entry in the middle, and hands it to me. "She says *D* took her there and calls it 'their spot.' It's this Fifties-style place just outside town. You know the kind I'm talking about? Stuck in time, and the waitresses still wear those cute dresses."

"McMullins!" The sudden outburst makes my head twist in Em's direction so fast there's a sharp pain that shoots through my neck. "That sounds like McMullins. It's, like, fifteen minutes outside the city. Cai took me there on a date once — oh, it's so cute! It has these adorable booths, the servers are *so* nice, and the burgers are as big as your face!" She crosses her legs and looks at me with one of the brightest, most genuine smiles I've seen in a long time.

I nod slowly. "Okay, so we check McMullins." I turn to Maddi. "I'm free tomorrow, can you get away? We can pick you up around noon."

"Sure, Dad picked up an extra shift tomorrow, so as long as I'm home before five, it should be fine," she says.

"Not a problem."

"Boo!" Em crosses her arms and pouts. "Sunday's are my date day with Cai."

"Oh, right. Well, I can fill you in after you get back."

Em lets out an overexaggerated groan before blowing a raspberry. "*Fine*, but I get to be a part of the next investigative portion! I wanna put these detective skills to the test!" She holds her fists in front of her face and punches the air in a one-two gesture. "Gotta catch them perps!"

"I'm switching you to decaf," I say.

"Rude!" She punches my leg.

"Ow!" I use my foot to push her backward.

After catching herself from falling, Em springs to her feet, smirks, and lunges at me. "Don't kick me!" She punches my arm a couple of times.

"Emerald!" There's faux anger in my tone as I push her off me. When she lands on the bed, papers scatter and slide across the floor. Before any of us can react, the door swings open and Mom's head pops into the room with a bright smile that fades when she sees Em and me.

"Is everything okay in here?"

"Fine, Mom," Em and I say in unison.

Em gets up from the bed, knocking more papers onto the floor, and lets out a frustrated growl. She looks at me after piling everything into a stack. "Desk?"

"Second drawer, thanks." I turn back to Mom. "What's up?"

"I was going to ask if Maddi was staying for dinner."

"No, but thank you, Mrs. Greene. I should be getting back home," Maddi says.

We collectively wait until Mom leaves before speaking again.

"Do you want to keep the journal here?" Maddi asks. "Read through everything?"

"Yeah."

Note to self: add everything Maddi told us to the notebook.

TWELVE

Days since Abi's disappearance: 14

It was another late night of staying up, but this time instead of studying or scouring a laptop, I'm able to relive the memories that Abi decided were good enough to highlight. I was able to learn about things through her eyes: how our dates make her feel, what she does to calm herself after disappointing news, what she enjoys about spending time with Em, Cai, and me. What I wasn't able to find, however, was any identifying information about *D* other than him being someone she trusts and thinks of as a friend. He's someone she enjoys spending time with, someone she can have in-depth conversations with, and someone consistent in her life.

After a run to Nero's Café for coffee, I head back home to settle at my desk with the journal, laptop, and notebook complete with my theories, frustrations, and questions.

Evidence:
Laptop. Search history: was searching for information about stalkers.

Journal. Unnamed individual became possessive and tried to take up Abi's time.

Car. Possibly white or tan, passenger side window squeaks when being rolled down.
Suspect List:
Jasper. Abi's science partner. Follows her around.

Michael Perkins. Abi's dad. Owns a white car, frustrated/angry with her for applying to BCC.

While reviewing my list of evidence and suspects, the conversation with Maddi about the night of Abi's disappearance replays in my mind. She mentioned going upstairs after dinner to study. If she did, couldn't that have given her father the ability to sneak out? The text conversation about milkshakes happened between nine-thirty and ten p.m. according to Maddi — something Mr. Jenkins confirmed.

If dinner was earlier in the evening, that would give them time for the movie before Maddi went to study. Dinner at five, movie at six, kidnapping at nine-thirty? I need to figure out when the fight happened, when dinner was, and how it all plays together.

Another thought occurs to me: could Maddi be put on the suspect list? She has access to the car too. She could've climbed out of her window without her father knowing and picked Abi up. That doesn't account for the _D_ initial, though, and Maddi is named in the journal in other passages. Why would Abi start using another label for her sister? Why would she be under the impression that her sister would be stalking her when they live in the same house?

That theory doesn't hold up, but her father...

I decide to table the thoughts about Mr. Perkins. After storing everything under my bed, I start getting ready for the day allowing my mind to wander back to Jasper. We don't know if he's been at school, we don't know for sure if he drives a white car, and we don't know where he was the night that Abi was taken. With too many unknowns, it's important for me to remember that every angle needs to be considered before coming to a conclusion.

It would be so easy to blame him. I could call the cops, say I have evidence, and make them investigate him.

The buzz of my phone draws my attention back to the present.

MADELEINE: STILL COMING?

Oh shoot!

ME: YEAH! SORRY. GIVE ME 10.
MADELEINE: ALL GOOD. I'LL BE ON THE PORCH.

After a shortened version of my morning routine, I throw on the first T-shirt and jeans I can find and run down the stairs.

"Good morning, Hu—" Mom pauses when she sees me rushing. "Is everything okay? What's going on?" Panic is bubbling to the surface when she bolts up from the couch. I've interrupted her morning ritual of reading with a cup of tea before starting whatever list she's made herself for the day.

When I catch sight of her, I pause and give her a smile. "Everything's fine. I'm going to meet Maddi for milkshakes, and I'm running late." It's not a lie. *Technically.*

I wait while she moves around the couch and comes over to me. She fixes the way my shirt lays on my shoulders, then waits for me to pull on my jacket so she can fix the collar of that too. She likes to pamper. I think it's because she likes to feel needed. She and Dad were very traditional in that way. She'd make the meals and send him off with a lunch and thermos of coffee every morning, and when he came home, she was waiting with dinner nearly finished and his favorite beer chilling in the fridge. Make no mistake, their marriage was far from perfect, but they had a good dynamic most days.

"Mom, please, I need to go," I say as I take her hands and press them together.

"Okay, okay. I'm sorry." She glances down, embarrassed.

My head dips so I can catch her eyeline and give her a more reassuring smile. "I'll text you when we get there, okay?"

She nods.

I'm at the door when she calls for me again. I turn, and she's twisting her hands in front of her. "I love you. Be safe."

"I love you too, Mom," I say before grabbing the keys and closing the door behind me.

My car is nothing special. It's a ten-year-old, dark green, two-door with dents and dings in random places where other cars have hit it. I call it *my* car, but it's one Mom gave to Em and me last year.

"Every kid should get a car for their sixteenth birthday," she told us, but Em was quick to point out that we didn't *each* get a car. We're supposed to share it — and we do — but I'm the primary driver. Perks of being the older brother. Whether Em likes to admit it or not.

***

"You're late," Maddi says as she slides into the passenger seat.

I wait until the door is closed, then take off down the road. "I overslept, then Mom was being, well, Mom."

She huffs, but the sound is muffled. When I glance her way, she's staring out the window.

Everything okay?

"Up late again?" she asks.

"Yeah, reading."

The journal.

"Gotcha."

The car is tense. I'm not sure if I'm reading into it too much or she's truly upset, but something in my gut says not to bring it up. The last thing we need right before we're supposed to be a team is to get into some kind of spat.

Do what Em always does: let it sit. If it's important enough, she'll tell you what's going on. It probably has nothing to do with you. She probably slept wrong or got into a fight with her dad about something. She's a girl. They get moody sometimes.

If Em were privy to my current thoughts, she'd probably slap me upside the head and go on some rant about how guys get just as moody as girls, but because we don't show emotions often, society doesn't recognize it.

I love Em, but when she gets preachy, she gets *preachy*.

THIRTEEN

Days since Abi's disappearance: 14

The diner is exactly like Abi describes in the journal. If you've ever seen *Riverdale*, it's pretty similar to where those kids go. Before you ask, I don't watch shows like that. It's another wonderful gift Em has given me during her rabbit-hole reading sessions that need background noise. I appreciate the aesthetic of the place even if it's not something I'd purposely choose. I enjoy more modern and quiet locations, but to each their own.

"It's adorable," Maddi says as we climb out of the car. "I'll have to come out here again one day."

You really want to come back to the place your sister was potentially kidnapped from?

I decide to keep the thought to myself and move around to her side of the car. After shooting the text to Mom that I'd promised her, I nod for Maddi to follow me inside.

It's not busy, but the few people that are here look like patrons. Older men and truckers, mostly. There's an even blend of stand-alone tables and booths with eight stools lining the bar. The vinyl on the seats don't show much age, but I can't tell if they're well taken care of or new.

I wonder how long this place has been here.

"Hi, welcome to McMullins!" The voice comes from my left and is so cheerful she could've been in a commercial. "Just the two of you today?" When I finally spot the hostess, she has a smile showing all of her teeth. Her bottle-blonde ponytail bounces as she springs toward us. She seems nice enough if you can get past the overly chipper nature.

How much caffeine have you had today?

"We're actually here to ask a couple questions?" I say, and her smile fades when my flat, unamused tone combats her earlier words.

"Ignore him." Maddi quickly pushes me to the side with her elbow and offers a mirror of the hostess' smile. I can't tell if she's being genuine or putting on a front. I've never seen a smile so wide from Maddi before.

What the hell was that, Madeleine?

"He's not always the most fluffy person to talk to," she says. "And, yes, we'd like a table, please."

"That's okay, I *completely* understand. I'm always a little grumpy before my morning coffee too," the hostess says before a giggle rings out that's so high-pitched it makes me cringe.

Bold of you to assume I haven't had my coffee yet.

"The name's Casey, by the way. Follow me." Her shining smile comes back at once. With another bounce on the balls of her feet, she gives a turn that resembles a twirl more than anything, and leads us to a booth in the back.

Are we sure it's caffeine she's on?

After we take our seats across from each other, Casey says, "Can I get y'all waters to start?" She hands us each an oversized, laminated menu with faded pictures of dishes they probably had professionally made to appear more appetizing.

"I'm fine for now," I say as I stare at the menu. The feeling of eyes burning holes into me hits me like a ton of bricks. When I look up, Maddi is staring at me with wide eyes.

Are you trying to scold me?

Normally I'm great at reading her facial expressions only this seems out of the ordinary. But, hey, at least she's not being moody anymore.

When she looks back at Casey, that bright smile is back. "That would be great, thank you." The two hold eye contact for a little longer than most people would consider normal, but eventually Casey nods and walks away. It becomes very clear what's going on when Maddi turns back to me.

Well, that's an interesting twist.

From the way Maddi looks at me, I can see the nervousness turning into self-consciousness. Her wide-eyed expression wasn't scolding me, it was her trying to tell me to be nice so Casey would stick around longer.

"I'm not going to judge you, you know." I turn back to the menu and search through the items I know I'm not going to buy.

"What do you mean?" Her voice is shaky. It's clear this isn't a conversation she's had with many people — if any — so I decide it's best to give her a little privacy and keep things vague.

"Your secret's safe with me. She's a little too valley-girl-meets-speedster for me, but, hey, I think you two would be a cute couple." I glance up and give her a playful smirk, then turn back to the menu. Based on the shifting from her side of the table, she's either sitting up or sinking into the seat to try to disappear.

"Th-thanks," she says, allowing excitement to quickly override the nervousness.

When I tilt the menu down, she's sitting taller, causing my smirk to settle into a soft smile.

Confidence looks good on you, kid.

"Does Abi know?" I ask.

The question catches her off guard. A flush of pink dusts her cheeks as she looks down at the menu again. "I've made hints, and she caught on, but we never said it out loud. I'm not sure how Dad will take it, so I've just never said anything to him about it."

Although I've never noticed any signs, I'm not surprised either. Maddi is a beautiful girl. She can easily have her pick of the guys in her grade, but I've never seen her so much as ogle any of them. Then again, I'm not someone who cares about the dating preferences of others so I hardly pay attention to that kind of thing. If it makes you happy, go for it. If it doesn't affect me, I don't care. Live your life.

"Hey, it's not my place to say anything. Besides, it's cute seeing you all — what'd they say in *Bambi*? Twitterpated?" I snort a small laugh. "If you think she's cute, it's worth a shot, so take it. Leave your number on the receipt before we leave." When I see Casey on her way back with a tray holding the water, a mug, and a pot of coffee, I sigh and sit back in the booth.

She's trying to be nice... she's trying to be nice... she's trying to be nice...

I know I shouldn't be annoyed, and I know she's probably trying to be considerate toward the cranky person at the table, but man is it irritating when people don't listen.

"I know you said you didn't want anything, but everyone deserves a good cuppa joe to start the day, right?" She sets the water in front of Maddi before pouring the coffee into the mug for me.

It's not the start of the day. It's after noon.

The smell instantly fills my senses and—

Okay, that smells delicious. Maybe it's not such a bad idea after all.

"Thank you, sorry about earlier. It's been a stressful week." My hands wrap around the mug. The ceramic is already scorching hot, but something about the sting of the heat is comforting.

"Aah, don't worry about it. It happens to the best of us." Casey looks between us, eyes lingering on Maddi before returning to me. "Y'all ready to order?" She gives me that irritatingly glowing smile again.

"I'm good with the coffee." I nod toward Maddi. "You?"

"Just a chocolate milkshake for now," she says. The confidence that started filling her is waning, and I can see she's retreating into herself again.

After jotting down the item on a notebook, Casey takes the menus and rests them on her hip. "Can I do anything else before I put the order in?"

Did we say we wanted anything else?

The moment the thought runs through my mind, I bring the mug to my lips for a drink. Clearly, I'm crankier than I thought. I can hear Abi's voice telling me to behave and not be so rude. She's part of the reason I've learned to keep things in my head more than I used to. "Every time you say something that should be kept in your head, you need to give me a quarter, Mr. Greene. Got it? No exceptions. You're a sweet boy, but you've got a mean mouth," she'd told me. It's a product of living and growing up with Em. When she first made the demand, I hated it, but after a few weeks, I started to understand: you don't get far in life with a "mean mouth."

"I was wondering if we could ask you a few questions," I say.

FOURTEEN

—◆—

Days since Abi's disappearance: 14

It's my turn to sit a little straighter in the booth as I take out my phone and pull up a picture of Abi and me. We're laying on our backs on the turf of the football field, laughing. It was so bright and sunny that day. I still remember the way her shampoo mixed with my cologne to remind me of a cold, misty, comforting morning. That moist, earthy, relaxing smell. I smile down at the screen as the memory settles in, then turn the phone to show her. "Do you remember seeing this girl?"

Casey pauses while she studies the photo, and hums in thought. The look of contemplation makes me miss the smile she had before. The longer she looks at the photo, the more a looming, dreadful feeling starts to settle in. What if she doesn't recognize Abi? What if this is a dead end?

"I think I remember her coming in — yeah! She was here... a couple weeks ago, I think. Yeah, m-hmm." She nods so quickly she resembles a bobblehead. I take that moment to put my phone back in my pocket. "She came in with a guy. You two know her?"

The moment she says she recognizes Abi, the dreadful feeling starts to lift and is replaced by a sliver of hope. "Yeah, I'm her boyfriend, she's her sister." I glance at Maddi, and we lock eyes on each other. I hope my expression reads as *I'm trying to help you*, but I force myself to turn back to Casey again before I know if Maddi understands. "Do you remember anything about that night? Did anything happen? Do you remember the guy? What he looks like? Or did she use a name?"

She remembers Abi. This is the diner she went to the night she disappeared, and it has to be the diner from the journal.

"Oh, man, okay." It's clear the list of questions is overwhelming her.

My bad.

"Um... they were a normal table for the most part. She — no, not really a name. She called him *D*, but that's all she referred to him as. I tried guessing his name, but they both just kind of smiled. It was weird though. She looked away when she smiled, almost like she was nervous or uncomfortable, and he... *stared* at me. You know when someone smiles, but you can see it's fake? Where it looks more menacing than inviting? One of those."

I should've brought my notebook so I could write this down.

She rolls her shoulders back in what I assume is an attempt to push the memory away and draws in a deep breath to continue. "Um, as far as what he looked like? He was a few inches taller than her and a dirty blond. Nondescript really. I'm sorry, I wish I could give you m—OH!"

The sudden outburst is startling.

Christ, woman.

"Hold on, I'll be right back! And I'll put in your order." With those words, she all but skips off toward the bar counter.

Maddi waits until Casey's out of earshot before turning toward me. "*D*. So she was *definitely* here with whoever that is, and that's who picked her up." Maddi leans against the booth's table while speaking. "How are we—" but she's cut off when I hush her.

Casey's already bouncing back over. "So, I will say that he gave me the heebie-jeebies. I thought they were a cute couple at first. When they came in, she was upset, but he kept trying to cheer her up. I assumed they got into some kind of fight in the car or something? The guy offered her anything on the menu, made jokes, and tried to hold her hand. She seemed like she wanted... I don't really know. Comfort, I guess? Space?"

She looks between the two of us, probably expecting someone to say something. When we don't, she says, "He got a little frustrated with her, but there wasn't any yelling or anything." She rummages in the front pocket of her apron, then pulls out a phone.

The moment I see it, adrenaline shoots through me. The way I spot Maddi is staring at me makes it feel like she can tell. I can recognize that phone anywhere; it's unmistakable. I've spent four years around it. Black phone case, paint spatter that's obviously added on after manufacturing, little letters — A&H — etched into the bottom-right corner.

That's Abi's phone.

"Why is that—how...." Forming proper sentences feels impossible, and I can't place whether it's rooted in anxiety or excitement.

This is why she wasn't answering the phone. Something's not right. Something happened.

"It was dropped on their way out. At some point she got—uhm—really tired?" Casey's eyebrows press together, it's obvious she's trying to figure out how to word things without it sounding as bad as it probably is.

Just tell us the truth. It's okay, we need to know.

"She was starting to slur her words, and she kept resting her head on her hand and closing her eyes. Don't get me wrong, I was glad she wasn't so upset anymore, but it didn't feel right. When the guy started to notice, he quickly asked for the check, slapped me a fifty on a twenty-dollar total, told me to keep the change and started trying to get her to stand up." Casey shifts her weight from one hip to the other. She's uncomfortable and I don't blame her. How do you say all of this without being affected?

"I wouldn't say she fought him, but she pushed his hand away at first and said she needed to call..." she pauses, thinking. "*Someone,* but I don't remember who."

Me — or Maddi. She knew something was wrong and was trying to get help. Oh god, Abi. What happened to you?

There's that sinking feeling in my stomach again, and as much as I don't want to admit what my mind is telling me — and the more Casey describes what happened that night — the clearer it's becoming.

Abi was drugged.

"Anyway, the phone was dropped when she stood up, and I guess they didn't notice. We hold all personal items for thirty days before disposing of them, so I picked it up when I was cleaning the table and kept it behind the counter thinking she'd come back for it. It was ringing off the hook the whole next day, then just stopped, so it might've died. If you guys know her — you're her sister, right?" She looks toward Maddi, but her smile is weaker than her earlier ones. Probably because of the heavier topic. No one expects to come to work and have to recount a situation like this.

Maddi nods.

"Then I don't think anyone would mind if I leave it with you. Make sure it gets back to her, okay? I don't want — I could get in trouble." A bell rings signaling an order being ready. "Oh, that's probably your milkshake. Back in a flash!" She springs off again.

"Is it still charged?" Maddi leans over the table again but glances over her shoulder to look for Casey instead of over at me.

I try the power button but the screen flashes to a red battery with a line through it. "It's dead. It'll match Em's charger though. We can head back and charge it at the house. I'll hold on to it there if you want."

It's probably better to keep the evidence together, and...

The thought of keeping Abi's things close brings comfort, but guilt trails along as well. It's not just me who's missing someone. Maddi is too. It's a thought I scold myself for not being more aware of. Abi's her sister. There are memories on the phone of them as much as there are of the two of us. I have a lot of things from Abi; clothes she's given me, notes I probably still have in scattered places around the room, text messages, pictures. Shouldn't Maddi be allowed to have something too?

It's a running record of her life. It has pictures my phone doesn't have of us. Memories, videos… technology saves people's lives. Freezes them in time so their loved ones can revisit who they were anytime they want. I'll be able to see her laugh and smile, hear her voice again, and if we never find her, this is all we'll have left.

The thoughts are scary and comforting at the same time, but they don't stop the 'what if' thoughts from barreling back. I push them away as best I can. We're getting clues, which means we're moving forward. Doing that means finding her and bringing her home.

"Sure," she says, although I can see the hesitation hiding behind her eyes. "Do you think we'll have time to look at things today?"

I glance at the large clock hung on the wall across the room. It took thirty minutes to get here and with talking to Casey, we've already been gone for nearly an hour and a half. "Depends on traffic, but, yeah, if we leave soon. It's almost two o'clock. I don't want to be the cause of *another* blowup with your dad."

Maddi waves off my concern and releases a hard sigh that makes her cheeks puff out. It makes me laugh.

"Ah, there's that lighter side of Hunter!" Her tease is accompanied by a nudge from her foot to mine under the table.

"Yeah, yeah. Whatever."

Before I can say much else, Casey arrives with the milkshake. "Heeere ya go!" When she sets it on the table, Maddi gives her an apologetic expression.

"I'm so sorry. Something came up and we have to take off. Can we have that to go?" she says.

Casey sniffs, causing her chipper smile to fade again, and nods in agreement. "Oh, yeah, sure. Let me put it in a to-go cup for you." When she leaves, she walks away without the signature spring in her step, and I realize how awkward it seems despite barely knowing her.

"Man, she was really hoping we'd hang out for a bit, huh?" My eyes watch Casey as she moves behind the bar counter to spoon the milkshake into one of those Styrofoam cups. "Maddi," I say, looking back at her, "do it. Leave your number for her." I nudge her foot like she did to me but straighten up again when Casey comes back over to set the check and cup down in front of Maddi.

"Thank you — for your time and answering all my questions." I give her my own version of her bright smile, but just like with Officer Samson, it feels foreign and awkward.

"Hey, no problem. I'm glad I could help. I hope she's okay," After a moment of silence, Casey draws in a deep breath and nods. "Well, you two have a good day, yeah? Come back and see us again soon." She twirls through half a turn and skips off toward the kitchen again.

Whirlwind of emotions, that one...

I wait for Maddi to drop her cash on the table, then slide out of the booth. "No phone number?"

"N-no." She's back to being her bashful self.

"Maybe next time." I usher her forward, but after getting halfway to the door, I pause and click my tongue.

No. Everyone needs a little push sometimes. It's been a crappy few weeks, and she needs something good to happen.

"Shoot," I say as I snap my fingers.

Maddi turns to me, confused.

"You head out to the car. I left my phone in the booth." She gives me a skeptical look complete with a head tilt and narrowed eyes. She doesn't believe me but doesn't call me out on it and continues walking. Once I'm sure I'm clear of her seeing me, I turn back to jog to the booth. I grab the pen Casey left with the check and jot down Maddi's phone number along with a small note: *Just text her.* When I turn to leave, Casey is looking at me with a raised eyebrow. I wink, and head back to the car.

In hindsight, she probably thinks the last interaction is bizarre. I greeted her with a less-than-favorable attitude, and when I did finally warm up, I start asking about a girlfriend, only to leave a note on the receipt.

You probably should've put something a little clearer on there, and what if Maddi gets mad at you?

Can't change it now.

FIFTEEN

Days since Abi's disappearance: 14

I'm hyperaware of Abi's phone in my pocket the whole ride back, but it's the swirl of questions in my head that distract me the most. What will we find when the phone is charged? Does it have a real name for *D*? What if it shows me things I don't want to see?

She has a stalker, not a secret boyfriend.

Sure, it isn't a secret boyfriend, but *D* is someone she trusts. What if they're someone I trust? What if I need to accuse someone I know? Someone I care about?

The more the questions invade my thoughts, the more my stomach knots, and the pounding in my ears causes pressure in my head, making me dizzy. The last time this happened was when Dad died, and I ended up passing out. I need to calm down. I can't pass out while driving.

It'll be okay. Breathe. This isn't like Dad. You'll find Abi.

But the thoughts and questions and worries don't wane, and the deep breaths aren't helping.

"Hunter." Maddi's tone is flat, annoyed. "Earth to Hunter. Hello?" When I look at her, I see she's turned in her seat to face me and is expecting a reply. How long has she been calling me?

"Sorry," I mumble and look back to the road just in time to pull into my driveway. After putting the car in park, I run my palms over the steering wheel and sigh. It's an attempt to let the tension go, but the shudder of my exhale gives away the anxiety still coursing through me.

The knots in my stomach tighten, and everything is unreal. I try to force my mind to focus on the way the leather of the steering wheel feels. It's old and there are cracks and tears in places from different hands and the heat of the sun. It's something I started doing after what happened with Dad: focusing on something using my senses. Em calls it "grounding." Whatever it's called, it usually brings me back to reality, but it's not working today.

All I can focus on is how everything could've been explained away until now: the journal entries, the search history, even the trip to the diner. The search history could've been for a project, or maybe she really did have a stalker but took care of it. What's clear is *D* exists. What I don't understand is if he's causing issues, why did she agree to go with him to the diner? Was it because they'd figured everything out and whoever it was accepted that they weren't going to get all of her time or be together? A question for another time. But this? The phone? Knowing that she was probably drugged? That someone took her away from the people she cared about?

I can feel my stomach tightening more, and I clench my jaw shut in case it tries to make me vomit.

I'm so glad there's nothing to bring up.

Maddi must see the change in my demeanor, because after silence fills the car, she lets out a heavy sigh and says, "Are you okay?" The annoyed tone from earlier is softer now.

"I don't— all of th—" I stop to let out another shaky breath while staring at the garage door in front of us. "None of this is what I expected." My hands rub against the steering wheel again, and the longer I look at the garage door, the more I realize how cracked and chipped the paint is. If I can focus on something other than my anxiety, things will be okay.

Oh no, you're going to open the flood gate. Don't do it, Hunter. Maddi doesn't need this. It's bad enough she's already seeing this little breakdown. You can't both be a mess.

"I didn't think we'd find all of this," I say. "I didn't think we'd find real evidence of her being taken." I scoff, but it's an attempt to push away the prickle at the corners of my eyes.

STOP. Hunter! You're supposed to be the strong one. You're supposed to make sure others are okay. Push this down. Breathe. You did it before, you can do it now.

But the thoughts continue before I can stop them. "She's gone. She's... missing." The words come out in a whisper so low it's almost inaudible, and part of me hopes she doesn't hear them. It's the first time I've said it out loud. I told myself from the start that if I don't say it, there is a chance that I'll wake up and this will all be a bad dream that went on for too long and everything will be okay, or I'll wake up to a text from Abi saying, "Good morning, see you soon, babe," and we'd meet on the football field like we always do. She'd run over, hug me, kiss me. Things would be okay.

I just want things to be okay.

I shake my head in disbelief. "I just don't understand why all of this is happening." I've held off letting myself process things so I can focus on collecting all the evidence. That's more important than breaking down and freaking out. Besides, Maddi needs me. She needs someone to be strong for her, to keep her going. We'll solve this, bring Abi home, and I'll deal with the emotions later. Em calls this "go mode" — when you push yourself to keep going and ignore things that can stop you. "I just need her to come home." My hands tighten around the steering wheel until my knuckles are white and the leather whines.

"Hunter...." Her hand reaches for mine, but I instinctively pull away. She lets out a heavy sigh; she's trying to find the right words to say.

You don't need to say anything. I get it. I'm bad at this stuff too.

"Please. You were there for me at the café, let me be here for you now. We need to support each other."

I don't know how to let you be there for me, and right now, I don't want to share my feelings. I don't want to be vulnerable and soft and open. I want to fight. I want to find Abi and bring her home. I want to find the bastard that did this and make sure he pays.

When she reaches for my hand again, I let her take it. Her skin is soft and warm, and for a moment, I find comfort in her touch. Flashes of the way Abi's hand feels in mine come to the surface. Gentle, reassuring, loving. As the thoughts settle in, my shoulders slump and my hand closes around Maddi's.

"I'm sorry," I say finally. The words come out defeated. When I close my eyes, a couple tears fall. Despite my best efforts, I can't stop them. With how little I cry and the lack of people who have seen me do so, everything about this moment feels wrong.

"Don't be sorry. This is what we're supposed to do." She squeezes my hand. "I'm here for you, okay? You don't need to be the big, strong guy all the time."

Yes, I do. It's my job. It's my job to protect those around me. If I'd been better at protecting Abi, she wouldn't be missing. If I'd have checked on Dad...

The conversation from the other day with Em replays. Maybe I am projecting. She's told me that I have a savior complex. She said it came around when Dad died because I couldn't help Mom. Watching her go through all of that was hard, of course, but knowing that I couldn't change it was worse. "You try to save everyone around you, Hunter," Em had said. I always told her she was full of it, but the further we fall down this rabbit hole, the more I think she's right.

I hate it when she's right.

I'm trying to save Abi, I'm trying to protect Maddi. I'm trying to make sure this has a happy ending.

"You miss her, I can see it." Maddi's voice waivers, giving away that she's starting to drown in her own emotions. "Your mask isn't as good as you think it is."

I huff out a laugh. "First of all, in the words of one Emerald Greene: *Rude.* Second, I appreciate it, but we need to stay focused." Every attempt to make the words sound kind fail, causing her to scoff.

"We're human, Hunter. I know you like to be the tough, scary guy, but we're allowed to be emotional. *You're* allowed to be emotional."

I'm aware of this, but it doesn't mean I want to be.

She pulls her hand away and twists her fingers around themselves. "Holding things in makes you hyper focus. If you don't process what you're going through, your brain will make you look *too* closely. And as with some mysteries, the closer you look at something, the less you see."

I pause at her last words and let my shoulders bounce in a silent laugh. "Okay, Sherlock. I get it."

"That was from a movie, actually."

I wipe my cheeks. "Okay, well, the therapy session is over. Let's go charge this phone."

Sixteen

Days since Abi's disappearance: 14

After grabbing Em's charger and plugging the phone in, Maddi and I settle on my bed with the cluster of collected items for what feels like the millionth time. At this point, I don't think there is a page or website I haven't read at least five times. "It's one of those fast-charging cords," I say, "so it shouldn't take very long." I grab the journal and start rereading the last couple entries. No matter how many times I read them, it still feels like I'm missing something.

Yeah, the truth, but she never wrote those answers down for you.

"I'm going to need you to relax." Her hand disrupts my view of the words before snatching the journal.

"I—"

"Aht-aht. You've been looking through all of this stuff for the last two days. Stop. Wait for the phone." As if on cue, the phone lights up between us. A cocky, triumphant smile settles on her lips that makes me roll my eyes.

The Perkins girls love being right.

I pick up the phone and it comes to life showing the lock screen. It's another picture of Abi and me. I'm kissing her temple as she looks at the camera mid-laugh. Memories of a picnic, tree-lined stroll, and Abi climbing a tree and almost falling while collecting wild crab apples all come flooding in.

Those crab apples were disgusting.

The evening ended with us sitting by the lake and talking. It was beautiful and quiet and serene and perfect. I smile at the screen, but it must look sad, because Maddi is moving to touch my thigh and get my attention.

"You okay?" she asks.

"Yeah, of course." I swipe up on the screen but pause when I see the numbers for a code pop up. "I... I don't know her code."

"Your birthday."

I don't show it, but I want to smile.

My birthday, that's cute. I probably never would've guessed that.

I tap *0-4-0-1* and a scattering of apps and folders litter the screen, covering another picture of us. This time we're kissing.

"Why do you know that?" I glance at Maddi then back at the phone. My thumb shifts over the screen to scroll through the different icons. Most are for filters or making art.

"We've always told each other. It's an 'in case of an emergency' thing," she says.

Guess it came in handy.

I nod while opening the text messages. My name is at the top and still holds my last message to her. I clear my throat and scroll down until I see *it*. The singular letter labeling a text thread. *D*. There is no hesitation in opening the thread and waving for Maddi to come closer.

ABIGAIL: I GOT INTO BCC, BUT HE'S SO ANGRY. I'M SICK OF THIS! WHY CAN'T HE JUST BE HAPPY FOR ME?

D: HE SHOULD BE. I'M HAPPY FOR YOU. AT LEAST YOU'LL STILL BE IN THE CITY. WE CAN STILL SPEND TIME TOGETHER.

ABIGAIL: IT WAS THE PLAN FOR ME AND HUNTER. BCC FOR PRE-REQS AND GEN ED COURSES, THEN WE'D FIGURE IT OUT FROM THERE. WE'VE TALKED ABOUT THIS. I'M WITH HUNTER.

D: I KNOW, BUT THERE'S NOTHING WRONG WITH US SPENDING TIME TOGETHER. BESIDES, YOU KNOW I COULD

MAKE YOU HAPPIER THAN HE DOES. I'VE PROVEN THIS TO YOU, HAVEN'T I?

D: ABS?

D: I'M SORRY, I'M NOT TRYING TO TURN THE CONVERSATION AROUND. IS HE STILL YELLING?

ABIGAIL: I LEFT.

D: WHAT? WHERE ARE YOU?

ABIGAIL: WALKING.

D: BUT WHERE? I'LL COME GET YOU. YOU SHOULDN'T BE WALKING AROUND ALONE AT NIGHT.

ABIGAIL: I'M FINE.

D: ABIGAIL, PLEASE. I'M SERIOUS. I'M WORRIED ABOUT YOU.

ABIGAIL: BOLTZ, BUT I'M FINE. REALLY. GOING TO GO FOR A WALK OR SOMETHING.

D: I'LL COME GET YOU. WE CAN GET MILKSHAKES AND TALK, OKAY?

D: ABS?

ABIGAIL: OKAY.

I look up from the phone and find Maddi biting her lip. The way her head is tilted down makes her hard to read. Is she disappointed? Confused? Hurt?

"Why didn't she call me?" Maddi wonders aloud. "I would've walked with her."

"She wanted to be alone," I say.

"...I guess."

I let silence take over the room for a minute.

"I wonder if this is around the time you text her."

"What's the time stamp?" Maddi asks.

I pull one of the bubbles to the side and see *9:00 p.m.* slide into view.

"It was a little before my text, but, yeah, I gave her some time — too much, apparently — to cool off. She must've been in the car already when I sent mine." That guilt is written on her face again. I find myself, again, wishing I could take it from her or say something to make it easier.

"So, she left around eight forty-five that night?" I ask.

"Probably. It could've been a little closer to eight-thirty, but the fight lasted a little while. I haven't seen them blow up on each other like that in a while."

I nod, then turn back to the phone and scroll upward, but pause when I see uppercase letters. The more I read what's on the screen, the more I have to force my breathing to stay steady. "Listen to this..." I say as I tap Maddi's arm.

ABIGAIL: I NEED YOU TO LEAVE ME ALONE FOR A LITTLE WHILE.

D: WHY?

ABIGAIL: THE NOTE IN MY LOCKER? THIS NEEDS TO STOP. I TOLD YOU, I'M WITH HUNTER.

D: BUT YOU KNOW HE'S NOT GOING ANYWHERE. YOU'RE WASTING YOUR TIME AND LIFE ON HIM!

D: ABIGAIL, YOU NEED SOMEONE WHO'S SMART, EDUCATED, SOMEONE WHO CAN MATCH YOU. I KNOW HOW SMART YOU ARE. I SEE YOU IN CLASS.

D: I'VE SEEN YOU TWO TOGETHER TOO — YOU AND HUNTER. IN THE HALLWAYS. HE DOESN'T LOVE YOU. HE'LL FIND SOME HUSSY GIRL IN COLLEGE AND LEAVE YOU. I CAN'T SEE THAT HAPPEN TO YOU. YOU DON'T DESERVE IT!

ABIGAIL: YOU SOUND LIKE MY FATHER. STOP.

D: ABIGAIL.

D: ANSWER ME.

D: STOP IGNORING ME.

D: LISTEN, FINE. YOU REALLY THINK I'M NOT GOOD ENOUGH FOR YOU?

ABIGAIL: IT'S NOT ABOUT THAT.

D: Isn't it? Why am I not good enough? I know you care about me. You leave me notes.

Abigail: Notes about class.

D: Yeah, but you don't leave them for anyone else. I know it.

D: Abs.

D: ABS.

D: Don't ignore me.

D: C'mon.

D: You're right. I'm sorry. I shouldn't have cornered you like that. You know how much I care. You know I get passionate about these things. I just want a good life for you. I want you taken care of. You have so much going for you.

Abigail: I want to build it my way.

D: Fine. I won't push it anymore, okay? Please meet me? Our place.

Abigail: You promise you won't bring it up again?

D: Yeah, of course.

Abigail: Okay. Our place.

SEVENTEEN

—•—

Days since Abi's disappearance: 14

"Well, that's concerning," Maddi blurts out and nearly rips the phone out of my hands.

"You're telling me. The way he's flipping? The way he completely goes off and then comes back down and is sweet again...."

"Why did she agree to meet with him?" She's scrolling up and down the thread as if it's going to give her the answer. The more we uncover, the more worried I'm becoming about what we'll find.

"She was probably nervous. Or afraid. I don't know, but it's someone she trusts, remember?" I grab my phone and bring up the dial pad. "Let me see that for a sec."

"What are you going to do?"

"I'm going to see if the line is still active." I click on the contact in Abi's phone and start dialing the number.

"WAIT!" She grabs my phone and pushes a series of buttons before handing it back. "*Now* dial the number."

An eyebrow raises as my eyes shift from my phone to her and back.

"So they can't catch who you are or what number you're calling from."

"Smart thinking." I call the number and hit the speaker button. Almost immediately, a horrid, high-pitched, squeal-like tone rings out, then an automated voice says the number dialed is disconnected or no longer in service. "Dang it," I mumble and punch the end button. "Is this really another dead end?"

"Who was that kid we were talking about the other day?" She pauses. "Jasper. Could this be him? I know I said I didn't really get that creepy vibe from him, but... you think he could be explosive like this?"

After rereading the texts, I think back to the suspect list. *D* is clearly not Mr. Perkins. She wouldn't talk about her father like that *to her father* and then agree to meet him at "their place". Wherever that is.

If D took her to the diner often or that's where they met up a lot, that's probably "their place."

"It's tough to say. The texts talk about notes for class, and we know from Em he's left notes in her locker. If he follows her around and leaves her notes, it's possible she found it uncomfortable enough to say she needed space."

"Okay. He could've twisted the notes saying she wanted to meet up for studying. I'm spit-balling — oh! What about the name in the phone? If it *is* Jasper, why would she label the contact *D*?" she asks.

It's a fair question, and to be honest, I haven't moved that far into the topic of Jasper being *D*. I'd worked through whether it was Mr. Perkins or Maddi, but Jasper...

I hold up my index finger before pushing off the bed and going over to my desk to grab a book out of the stack piled there. I've always thought yearbooks were stupid. You pay all this money for a book of pictures, and for what? Most people aren't in the majority of the photos; it's filled with people you don't care much about. There's faculty and staff, and popularity contest winners are placed in made-up categories. In a couple of years, you barely remember the people in your class... hell, you probably won't even talk to them anymore. However, Mom always says they're memory savers. "Get people to sign it, and you'll look back on it when you're my age and laugh about all the fun things that get brought up by reading about your old friends," she always says.

Seems like the yearbook came in handy finally. Thanks, Mom.

When I sit on the bed again, I flip it to the junior class section.

Our town is a moderate size, but people don't move here out of the blue for no reason. When you move to Bakersfield, it's because of family, for a very specific job, or you're trying to start over where absolutely no one knows you. If you make it to high school in this town, you've usually been here for a while. Logic tells me that Jasper has been going to our school for at least a couple of years.

"He should be here somewhere," I say, mostly to myself. After a few more flipped pages, I poke my index finger at a picture and turn the book toward Maddi. "Aha! Jasper *DeFoe*."

When she takes the yearbook to get a closer look, I grab my notebook off the bed and start updating the evidence and suspect lists.

Evidence:

Laptop. Search history: was researching information about stalkers.

Journal. ~~*Unnamed individual became possessive and tried to take up Abi's time.*~~ *Evidence D is the stalker being researched on the laptop, D found a diner that's known for milkshakes (where she was taken the night she disappeared?), D is someone she trusted.*

Car. Possibly white or tan, passenger side window squeaks when being rolled down.

Cellphone. Text exchanges with D. Erratic behavior, talks about "their place."

Suspect List:

Jasper DeFoe. Abi's science partner, follows her around, drives a white car (?), last name has the same first initial as the code name in Abi's phone.

Mr. Perkins. Abi's dad. Owns a white car, frustrated/angry with her for applying to BCC. (Maddi says they were both home all evening.)

I'm so busy updating the lists that I'm not aware of Maddi reading over my shoulder until she sniffs once. It's one of those dry sniffs that signal more annoyance than tears. It makes me pause writing and look at her.

"Okay, first, that sounds like a villain name." Her voice is slow and lazy sounding as she reads. There's a moment of silence, then a disgruntled noise that I can't place. "And second, my *father*, Hunter? Really?"

She's scowling at me.

Ouch. I didn't expect that big of a reaction.

"To be fair, I was going to put you on there too. Even you said cops always look at those closest to the victim first. Your dad would be *numero uno* with the fact that the two of them fought so often *and* right before she went missing. You guys own a white car, and with you being each other's alibis? Maddi, even you said you went upstairs to study, which means you weren't with him all evening. There was a time when he was alone. Either one of you could've taken the car, grabbed Abi, stashed her somewhere temporarily, and gone back later. As long as both of you have the same story, you both have a reason you *couldn't* be there."

She scoffs in disbelief. It's a theory I haven't fully believed from the get-go, and the more evidence we find the more outlandish it seems, but, like I said before: all angles, right?

"Are you serious? You think I could've done something to my sister or covered for my father if he did?" I watch her shift from disbelief to anger.

"Maddi, calm down. I'm saying it could've been a valid theory. Do I think you did it? No, but objectively speaking, it's something that I did and had to think about. There's means, motive, and opportunity. Your dad has been quiet about Abi since all of this went down. He could be seen as a father who's too nonchalant about his daughter being missing—"

"You haven't seen how much he's thrown himself into his work to avoid being home." The anger in her voice makes her words venomous.

"I know, I've been doing the same thing, remember? I haven't studied for finals at all since all this started. I've been doing *this*." I gesture to the assortment of items surrounding us. "The other day was the only day I've tried to study, and I didn't get very far. Like I said, do I think you guys did it? Or one of you? No. Was there reasonable suspicion? Yes, but the texts on the phone prove that it wasn't your dad. Or you."

I'm trying to help the situation. I need to de-escalate it before things go sideways. I really don't want to fight right now. It won't help either of us and will just make this whole thing harder.

"Those texts talk about leaving notes, right?" I ask.

She stares at me with hard, intense eyes. *The Perkins Stare.* It sends chills through me and makes my jaw clench. "Yes."

"Okay. How would she leave notes for your dad other than on the fridge or somewhere in the house? And even taking the note thing away, the part about giving her a better life and being with her? C'mon, Maddi." The corners of my lips pull in to form a thin line while my eyebrows scrunch inward to give her an *are you kidding me?* expression.

She closes the notebook and swats me with it before opening it again. "Yeah, okay, you're right. But don't you *dare* accuse us of hurting Abi again. Never in my life...." She looks at the notebook and reads over Jasper's mini profile. "I'll admit, he fits a lot of things so far — oh! Didn't Casey talk about the guy Abi was with being a little taller and dirty blond."

I nod then gesture for her to hand the notebook over so I can add it to the list.

"That fits him too," she adds, "and if you didn't want people to figure out who someone was when you're talking to them, you'd use something that would be a little obscure — I would anyway."

"That was my thought too, but why would Abi want to keep talking to Jasper a secret if they were just partners for class?" I'm trying to be practical, skeptical, and look at every side. Is Jasper suspect number-one right now? Yeah, of course, but he's also the *only* real suspect.

"I don't have an answer for that one," she remarks as she looks over my shoulder at the notebook again. "I think we're getting to the point where we need to confront him to know more things for sure."

Her words snap me out of my thoughts. "What?"

"We need to confront Jasper soon. Find him at school, make him talk. We need answers." For someone who's usually so timid, Maddi has sure found a backbone in the last couple of weeks. "If he did take Abi, he's not going to come out and say it."

"Wow."

"What?" she asks.

"I've never seen you do that. Take charge, be so assertive."

"I'm not spineless." She picks up Abi's phone and opens the photos to look through them. Despite the strength in her words, I can see the pain in her eyes as she scrolls. "I want to find her as much as you do, but if Jasper confesses, we need to go to the cops. We can't keep taking this on by ourselves. There's a process for all of this."

"I know." Do I agree with going to the cops first? No. They're useless, and I'd rather find Abi *then* go to the cops and have them arrest whoever did this. They weren't interested in following their little 'process' before. Hard evidence is the only thing they seem to listen to, but how will we be sure we have enough? It's easier to save Abi first, be a first-hand witness to the fact that she's found in a specific place that ties whoever did this to her to that location. That's a topic for another time though. "Have you been watching those detective shows?" I ask in an attempt to bring a lighter feel to the conversation again.

She glances up at me with a coy smile then back down at the phone. "*Maaaaybe.*"

We both laugh.

Suspect List:

<u>*Jasper.*</u> *Abi's science partner, follows her around, drives a white car (?), last name has the same first initial as the code name in Abi's phone, blond, taller than Abi.*

~~<u>*Mr. Perkins.*</u> *Abi's dad. Owns a white car, frustrated/angry with her for applying to BCC. (Maddi says they were both home all evening.)*~~

EIGHTEEN

Days since Abi's disappearance: 15

Em ended up spending the rest of the day with Cai — which isn't surprising, their date days are just that, *days,* especially now that he's attending college — but it meant that she didn't come home. Mom's never happy when that happens, but she also understands that we're teenagers and, well, Em is less likely to listen if the leash is tugged on too tightly. Dad was always the one convincing Mom to let us "go be teenagers," and after he died, our already short leash was yanked on and cut shorter. I try to remind Em to go easy on Mom, but she's stubborn and independent. They're exactly the same in that regard.

However, this is the one time I was hoping she'd actually come home. Now, I either have to wait until I see her at school and risk talking about everything in front of the potential kidnapper or wait until we get home. Neither option is preferable, but I need her thoughts on things.

Knowing that there is a very real possibility that we can catch this person and they're someone likely roaming the school's halls makes me look at everyone differently. Every corner seems mysterious, every glance feels menacing.

I pause in the doorway of Mr. Clarke's room long enough to spot Jasper sitting two seats behind Em, then head over to the seat she's saving for me.

"How'd it go?" She hunches her shoulders and leans toward me when I sit in the seat next to her. "Did you guys find anything?"

So much for waiting until we get home, I guess.

When Em wants to know something, she's relentless, and I don't have the energy to fight her off right now.

I mirror her hunch and nod. "A waitress was there that night and told us what happened. She had Abi's phone too—oh, by the way, your charger is in my room."

She twirls her wrist and rolls her eyes to wave off the mention of the charger. "What did you guys find out? Was there anything on the phone?" The more questions she shoots at me, the faster she talks, and the faster she talks, the louder she gets.

"Sh, *Em.*" I glance over my shoulder, then back to her. I don't need her bringing unwanted attention, especially with Jasper so close by.

"Sorry."

"It's fine. I'll fill you in more at home when we're all together, but from what we found, I'm pretty sure it's who we were talking about the other day. It'll make more sense when you have everything in front of you." The last part of the sentence makes my heartrate pick up again. If it links up, we can find her. If we find her, we can save her. "Maddi thinks we need to confront him soon, but I need muscle in case something goes down."

"I've got your muscle right here, bucko." She holds up her right arm and flexes while slapping her bicep with her other hand, that toothy grin forming again.

With a scoff, I shake my head. "You're so dumb—but, yes, I was going to say you should come with me. He might play quiet, and *no one likes me so I'm not a threat,* but if things turn sideways, I need my right-hand girl with me."

Her smile disappears and is replaced by a scrunch of her nose and her upper lip pulling back. "Thanks for thinkin'a'me, broski. Can't wait to see ev—" Her words are cut off by the clearing of someone's throat. We look toward the front of the class at the same time.

"This isn't social hour you two." Mr. Clarke points toward my desk, pauses, then straightens his back. "Actually, who wants to run an errand for me? Since neither of you are doing your work, it's not like it'll be disrupting anything."

That's a gross attitude, and why are you pointing at only my desk? We were both talking.

"I will." Em stands then turns to me. "You need to focus on schoolwork more than me." She tries to keep her voice down, but it doesn't seem to matter because Natalia Duran still glances over her shoulder and spits a sharp *sh!* our way.

I pull out a notebook and my copy of *Wuthering Heights*. Despite my desire for some time out of the classroom, Em looks like she needs the time away more than me.

"Thank you, Miss Greene," Mr. Clarke says while handing her a piece of paper and the hall pass before turning back to whatever he's been working on at his desk.

"Yeah, don't mention it, Teach." She gives him a sarcastic, two-finger salute and turns on her heel to leave.

Once she's gone, Mr. Clarke turns his gaze back to me. He stares and I stare back, but after a moment I can see his bottom lids squint upward.

Is he trying to read me? Intimidate me? Is he suspicious of something?

I mimic his expression. It's hard to read him, and that alone is off-putting. He seems annoyed, angry.

Why?

"Your book report, Mister Greene." The tone he used with Em was appropriately stern, so why does the one toward me sound almost hostile?

"Right, sorry," I say, but my eyes linger on him.

That was... odd.

When Em returns, she looks more annoyed than when she left. "You know," she says as she slides back into her chair and rummages through her bag, "it makes no sense why the school still does the whole *manual attendance* thing."

I glance up from the paragraph I'm writing to see her sarcastic smile. After marking my page, I turn to look at her and sigh. "Oh, is that what he had you take?" My eyes slide toward Mr. Clarke's desk to see if he's paying attention. I don't feel like getting yelled at — or glared at — again.

"Yeah." She slaps her own copy of *Wuthering Heights* down on the desk, eyes focused in Mr. Clarke's direction. "Couldn't he take it at the end of the day? Better yet, there's that cool thing called *email*... or maybe take it himself." She turns back at me. "We're not kindergarteners, we can manage by ourselves for five minutes." Her notebook is the next thing to assault her desk. "Instead, he gets to sit at his desk and write in that planner of his."

Ah, it was a planner, got it.

"If you have something you'd like to share, Miss Greene, I'd be happy to listen." That stern, flat tone is back. When he raises his head, he peers at Em, over to me, then back to Em.

I pause.

What was that?

I can't be sure, but it looked like the scowl from earlier came back for a split second.

"Nope. I already said what I needed to." She flashes him a strained grin with squinted eyes, and I wait to see him give her the same look he'd given me... but it doesn't happen.

What the hell?

Nineteen

Days since Abi's disappearance: 15

In between classes, Em and I discuss how and when to confront Jasper. With Abi already having been gone so long, it's becoming increasingly more important that we find her. What condition is she being held in? What if she's not being cared for? What if she's hurt?

"How should we do this?" Em asks while leaning against the locker next to mine.

I take a moment to think over a couple of options while switching out my textbooks. "I don't want to corner him if we can help it. He'll end up panicking, and if he really is as dangerous as the person from the texts seems to be, I don't want to see what he does when he's desperate."

"Fair... Well, we know he's at school today. One of us could keep tabs on him: see what he does, where he goes, if he talks to specific people."

After zipping up my bag, I close the locker and look at her. "I can do that. You've got that bio test, don't you?"

Em lets out a sigh that puffs out her upper lip.

"If I say no, can I do the fun things too?" Her tone sounds more like a grumpy child than her normal self. When she crosses her arms over her chest with a pout, I roll my eyes and push her along the hall.

"C'mon, let's go. You need a good grade so you can try to catch up to me with that GPA of yours."

"Ew, it's only .3 below yours. Don't be rude."

"Three minutes too slow to our birth and .3 weaker in school. At least you have your looks, kid." The pat to the top of her head that accompanies my words earns an elbow to my gut.

"I'd rather be good-looking. Don't need to be smart if they're distracted."

A groan-based laugh surfaces. "Yeah, yeah. Good luck on your test."

It's not a lie that I want Em to go to class for her test, but my main reason for volunteering is to see things myself. Of course, I trust my sister, and she's proven herself more than capable of being sneaky to get information in the past, but all of this is too personal now. That, and I have a hard time not being in control — according to Em. She always reminds me "it would've gone smoother if you let people help," but if that's not the pot calling the kettle black. I've never met someone more "I can do this myself" than her.

I'm halfway through Spanish class when I spot Jasper walking passed the door. I can't see much through the small, square window, but I can see him glance over his shoulder as he walks by. Is he being followed? Why does he look worried?

What are you up to?

"*Señor Greene,*" a female's voice says.

I immediately turn my head back toward the front of the class and give Mrs. Vélez a smile. "*¿Sí?*" She's unimpressed with both my smile and nonchalant answer.

"Is there a reason you're not paying attention?"

"*Lo siento, Señora Vélez,*" I shift in my seat to fully face the front again. "Uhm, actually, can I run to the restroom?"

She gives me the once-over, probably to size me up and figure out what ulterior motive I have while also deciding whether to make me ask again in Spanish. Eventually, she nods and points to the hall pass hanging by the door.

"*Gracias.*"

Once in the hallway, I make sure to keep my steps as quiet as possible. I lost which way Jasper went when Mrs. Vélez pulled my attention away from the door, but there are only so many places he can go. The high school isn't very big. It's a long, rectangular building, and has two floors with a few classrooms on each side of the hall, a football field that doubles as a soccer field, and a baseball diamond. We have a few hundred students, but it's tiny compared to other places.

Check the bathrooms first.

My Spanish class is on the first floor, leaving two possible bathrooms for Jasper to go to. The closest one is down the hall on the right, so I decide to stop there first. The door creaks as I push it open, and I find myself silently cursing the old hinges. If someone wanted to sneak up on another person — you know, like right now — it would be impossible. Luckily, when I'm able to see the stall and rest of the room, it's empty.

"Where—" I cut myself off and let out an exasperated sigh while looking up at the ceiling. I have a limited amount of time to figure this out, and I'm wasting time not being strategic.

We have two more classes before the end of the day, and I can practically hear Em screaming about how she should've skipped her test to follow him. The kid's sneaky, I'll give him that. Even if he's not trying, with how quiet he is and how much he keeps to himself, he has the luxury of being able to slip by people without being noticed. In a school where everyone knows everyone to some degree, that's a feat in and of itself.

It's easier to wait until after school.

Is all of this worth the risk of getting in trouble? If I'm caught in the hallway longer than I'm supposed to be, I could get detention or suspended. Mom will kill me if that happens again. As good as she is at it, she doesn't like having to be the hard-ass parent who disciplines, and I can tell that it upsets her when she needs to be.

Just try the other bathroom. If you stand here and mull over ideas of where he could be, you'll just waste all your time.

I double the pace of my steps and continue down the hall toward the next bathroom, but when I round the corner to the staircase, I immediately turn back around and hide. With my back pressed against the wall, I stare forward and wait, listening. When I poke my head around the corner again, *he's* there about thirty feet down the hall.

Jasper.

He's just standing in front of Abi's locker.

What... what are you doing?

The locker is still covered in pictures and notes and handmade cards and dying flowers. There's a teddy bear or two sitting on the ground in front of it with a few unlit candles that some of the cheerleaders thought would be a cute symbol for "lighting the way to bring her home." When they put them there, I had to work really hard not to remark on how fake it was. They hate Abi — always make fun of her when they can — but when you want to look like a sympathetic and understanding person who's not a complete witch-without-the-W every other day of the week, I guess you make grand gestures that don't mean anything.

Everything in me screams to confront him here and now, but this might be the only time I really get to see what he's like without him noticing. People are always their most authentic self when they think they're alone, and that's exactly what I need from him right now.

Jasper reaches into his pocket and pulls something out, but I'm too far away to see what it is. What I do see, however, is him pushing whatever he took out of his pocket through the grate in the locker.

So, you do leave her notes... but are they the notes that the texts talk about?

If they are, why is he still leaving them? Em's voice in the back of my head tells me it could be part of his obsession. He really can't handle being at school without her. Doesn't matter that he has her stashed somewhere and can go visit her whenever he wants, school is still torturous for him without her here. The mere idea makes my blood boil, and the tightness in my chest that comes along with the rise in blood pressure tells me it's based in anger, not anxiety, this time.

I'm going over what to say to him in my head and about to step away from the corner when I stop.

Someone's coming.

A teacher. She's short with blonde hair and touches Jasper's arm when she's close enough. I can't make out what they're saying, but I know that kind of touch anywhere, she's a mom. Whatever she says to him causes him to shrug off her hand and take a step back.

Who are you? Why are you comforting him?

I watch her say a few more things and walk away, but instead of going with her, Jasper turns back to the locker. His hand presses to the metal for a minute, then he straightens some of the papers and cards. He's getting ready to leave. If I don't move soon, I'm going to miss my chance to talk to him. I see the familiar slump of his shoulders form, but before he turns to walk away, Jasper glances around. What I see next causes a knot so sudden and disastrously tight I cover my mouth to stop myself from shouting. Slowly, he leans toward one of the photos and kisses it.

He's not grieving her. He's visiting her.

I feel sick. Does he see her locker as a shrine? Is he feeding off of everyone's sorrow from her disappearance? Standing at her locker when no one's around for his little fix? My heart is racing so fast I can hear that pounding in my ears again. I should yell at him, tell him how sick he is for what he's done, but all I can do is stare. Stare as he walks away like nothing's happened. As if he's done nothing remotely wrong.

He did this. I know he did.

TWENTY

Days since Abi's disappearance: 15

I can't focus the rest of the school day. My mind is fixated on what I saw and what it all means. I need to know *why* he took her and why he's not letting her come home. The plan was to just observe, but observing isn't getting us anywhere. We need action, and if I can get him to talk today, I'm going to. When the final release bell rings, I'm out of the class before Ms. Fitzgerald can give us the homework assignment.

Note to self: grab the assignment from Em later.

Keeping up with him through the crowds of students rushing to leave is simple enough, but he's far enough ahead that I almost lose him once we're in the parking lot. I'm pushing through a crowd of jocks when I notice him looking through his bag. This is my chance. I can close the space, I can catch up. I can stop him.

"Hunter!" The female voice behind me is shrill enough to make me turn out of instinct. It isn't panicked, but the urgency is evident. A girl with brunette hair in spiral curls comes sprinting toward me.

Octavia Michaels. Great. Now what?

"Hey, sorry. I forgot to give you your notes back from Science class. I know how you are with your studying." She's pulling out a tattered notebook and handing it to me. "Wouldn't forgive myself if you couldn't start with all that early finals prep, y'know?" She nudges me with a giggle. It's the same noise Em once called

Octavia's 'desperate, flirtatious giggle'. There's a pause that makes her smile wane when I don't respond in kind.

A glance over my shoulder shows Jasper getting into a car and pulling out of the parking spot. A frustrated growl rumbles at the base of my throat.

Crap.

"Why do you study so early anyway? Finals aren't for another month or so."

"As much as I'd love to sit here and discuss the logistics of why it's better to study a little at a time instead of trying to cram a bunch of information all at once, I need to go. Thanks for the notebook."

"Everything okay?"

"Yes. Fine." With the notebook shoved into my backpack, I let out a short, irritated exhale.

"But I—"

"See you in class," I say before immediately turning and heading toward my car. I could've been nicer, I could've made small talk or even made my words sound more appreciative, but she stopped me from getting to Jasper. I had a clear opening to end all of this, and *Octavia Michaels* managed to ruin it.

At least I know one thing: Jasper *does* drive a white car.

Maddi comes back to the house with Em and me so we can fill Em in about what Maddi and I learned at the diner. It doesn't take long to explain, but the few minutes of heavy silence that sit between us feels like an eternity. It's becoming a reoccurring theme. I stare at Em as she processes. She's mulling over the information, trying to piece things together the best she can. So far, we have some text messages, a couple witness accounts, and confirmation that Jasper — who fits the description of the person from the diner — drives a white car.

"So, based on what this waitress said, you think she was drugged?" Much like the last time the three of us were in my room, Em is on the ground, feet propped up on my bed, with a pillow under her head.

"It's possible," I say.

"I mean, it does make sense. No one shows up to a diner upset and ends up stumbling out without a reason." The way she looks up from the spot she's been fixated on reminds me of an animatronic coming to life: robotic and calculated.

"My thoughts exactly," Maddi says, then turns to her phone, smiles, and starts typing. This has been a normal occurrence for the last few days, but I haven't had time to ask her about it. "By the way…" She pauses until her text is sent, then looks at me. "Casey texted me. Don't do that again…." She puts on a frown, but the annoyance doesn't reach her eyes. "…But also… thank you." A smile slowly creeps across her features showing me that the giddy girl from the diner is back and thriving somewhere inside of her again.

Happy to help. I'm just glad you're smiling again.

It's a selfish thought, and one that comes because I don't know how much more heaviness I can handle. At least if Maddi is distracted by something else, I can focus on finding Abi and not keeping Maddi out of her own head.

"Noted, and you're welcome." I nod, then turn to Em. "It's a safe bet to say Abi was drugged. Especially if she wasn't accepting of his advances." I grab the laptop, journal, phone, and notebook from under my bed. "Whoever this is, they wanted her time and attention, and when she didn't willingly give that to him, he took it into his own hands."

Although we don't have proof of someone slipping Abi something, it makes sense given what Casey saw. I hate the idea of someone taking advantage of her like that. Even more, I hate the idea of what those types of situations usually lead to.

Maddi takes Abi's phone, unlocks it, and starts scrolling while I open the notebook.

Em lifts her head and looks between Maddi and me. "And we're absolutely set on Jasper being the guy? Sure, he drives a white car but he could just be crushing on Abi."

I nod. "He fits what Casey described, he's left notes for Abi before, his last name starts wi—"

"Hey, Hunter...." Maddi glances up from the phone, seemingly unaware of the fact that the conversation had continued around her. "Do you remember this day?" She hands the phone to me.

The picture she presents is Abi and me again. It was a day the two of us decided to abandon all responsibilities, skip school, and go hang out at a local park. I smile as I stare at it. Our eyes are squinted from the sun, but Abi's smile outshines anything else in the photo. "Yeah, why?"

Maddi leans around the side of my shoulder so she can see the screen and swipes through a few different photos. I watch and try to study each scene Abi captured, but I can't see any common tie. She scrolls through pictures of Abi and me laughing, kissing, and, at the end, pictures of scenery from various places from that date. "Maddi, I don't... I don't know what I'm supposed to be seeing here."

She sighs while taking the phone. After zooming in on the right-hand side of one picture, she shoves the phone back to me. "*That.* Right there." In the corner, and barely visible, sits a white car with a figure in jeans, a baggy hoodie, and a hat leaning against the hood. The figure and car are out of focus, but it's obvious whoever this is was watching, having turned to face Abi and me.

There's no way.

When I remain silent, she takes the phone back, swipes to the next picture, zooms in to the left side, and turns the phone to me again. It's a different angle, but it's definitely the same car — I'm sure of it.

"What is going on up there?" Em pulls her legs from the bed and sits cross-legged with her hands in her lap. "Care to share with the class?" I try not to let it show, but the expression she uses makes me wince, and I'm suddenly transported back to English earlier today with Mr. Clarke and his scowl. It's not to the same caliber, but it still causes my stomach to churn.

"Apparently Maddi found someone with a white car in a couple of photos."

After pushing up from her place on the floor, Em sits next to me to look at the phone. "There are probably thousands of white cars in the city. You think *this* is the person that took Abi? When were those taken?" she asks while tapping the screen to bring up the date and time with a few other details. "That's from almost three months ago... and during a *school day*." Em pauses to give me a *seriously, Hunter?* expression before continuing. She doesn't need to tell me the look is in regards to the skipping of school and not the idea of whether someone was following us.

Was this the day I ditched lunch with her? Oops.

"You think the stalker has been following her that long? That they skipped school and followed you around all day?"

"It might not have started out as bad as it got," Maddi says.

She has a point. What if this was when *D* was only starting to get possessive and stalk her? Was this when she still felt safe and secure with him? What if Abi didn't even *know* that's what he was doing yet? They could've followed her — us — for months before either of us knew or found out.

Maddi takes the phone back and swipes to the first photo and zooms in again to show Em. "It's fuzzy, but..."

Em stares at the phone longer this time. Her expression is blank, but I know her well enough to see her trying to connect the dots. She's probably running through a list of who that could be and if she's seen them around before. "Quality aside, does that look like a skinny, quiet kid to you guys? Jasper borders on scrawny, probably a buck forty soaking wet. This guy — yeah, okay, he's wearing a hoodie and a hat — definitely looks beefier to me." She hands Maddi the phone and grabs my notebook. "Let's step back from Jasper and look at things again, start over a little, because if that really is the guy that took Abi, I think we're going in the wrong direction."

"He could easily just be hiding in the clothes. People wear clothes that are too big for them all the time. Plus, I've been trying to think of other people, but nothing else really lines up." I hand her a pen, then lean back against the wall.

"It's possible, but it never hurts to expand the circle of possibility. If we pigeonhole ourselves too soon, we won't be able to solve this properly," Em says.

I have to work hard to not roll my eyes. It's obvious who took her, at least to me.

"Let's start with everyone who has blond hair, goes to our school, and is most likely to converse with Abi on a daily basis." Em turns the notebook to a clean page.

"There's Jesse Barnum." Maddi doesn't sound sure, but Em writes his name down anyway. "He's a senior with you guys. Abi told me he's in her math class."

"Tatum Jones? Varsity football. He has homeroom with us," I say.

The pen scrawls across the paper in neat, cursive lettering. "What about Mr. Clarke?" Her tone is teasing, but it still makes me pause.

"Very funny," Maddi says with a roll of her eyes.

"I—" I pause. Is it a good idea to bring us down this road? I'm probably reading too much into it.

But what if it is him, and you pushed the idea away and lost your chance to find Abi?

What if it's wrong, and it accuses an innocent man? The idea that all of this could destroy someone's life if they are wrongfully accused slaps me out of nowhere.

Did this person think about ruining Abi's life? No. Besides, what happened to looking at every possibility?

"He might be a good person to add to the list. He fits physically, Abi and he were close — she loved English class — and he..." I pause, clench my jaw. This is it. If what happened is going to be brought up, it needs to be now. "...He was behaving weird in class today. You know when someone doesn't like you, but they don't say anything? You can just *feel* it? When you left to take that note to the office, he squinted at me."

They're both staring at me. It's uncomfortable and awkward and I'm suddenly very aware of how faded my current pair of jeans are. Even I can admit that it probably sounds dumb, but isn't Em always the one that says to trust your gut? My gut is telling me something about him might be off.

"Squinted. Hunter, really?" Em asks in a sarcastic tone.

"Shut up. I'm trying to figure out how to describe it. There was this *look* like he couldn't stand the sight of me. Call it intuition, but something felt off, and in the texts, *D* talks about me not being good enough and him being able to give her a better life. It sounded like he already *could* do that. If that's true, maybe he's older and established."

"That... seems like a stretch." Maddi says. "There's no real evidence linking him to Abi outside of school."

"There's no *real evidence* linking Jasper to her outside of school either, but we're still loving him as suspect number one — look, I'm just saying it felt off and, right now, we have as much information that could lead us toward Mr. Clarke as we do Jasper." My eyes bounce between Maddi and Em, and the longer I look at them, the more the confidence in my theory waivers.

"He was probably irritated that we weren't doing the work," Em says.

With a deep inhale, I release a heavy sigh and look toward the ceiling.

Just let it go. Don't be so sensitive.

I mull everything over again. "Yeah, you're probably right. It was just a thought."

"Okay, moving on. We have Jasper DeFoe, Jesse Barnum, Tatum Jones..." Em rereads the list again before writing down another name. "I'll put Mr. Clarke on here too. He *does* match what you guys described, and I guess he could fit the build of the guy in the phot—OH! What side of the car is visible in those photos?"

Maddi looks at the phone again. "It's really fuzzy—ugh, I hate portrait mode." She gives a frustrated sigh, then hands me the phone.

I tilt my head to the right while looking at the screen. "The trunk is visible in this one."

"Perfect," Em says.

"Why?"

"Can you make out the plate?"

I turn the phone a little and straighten my head. "A? Is that a 4? K? No—an R?"

"Oh my *god*, give me that." Em snatches the phone from my hands and follows the same head tilt and phone turn motion. "The second character in? That's *definitely* an R." She squints her eyes as if that will sharpen the photo. After giving up on trying to make out whatever letters and numbers are hidden in the image, she sets the phone down then writes the R in the second space of six lines on the page.

"Sooo... what's the next step?" Maddi asks.

"Well," Em taps the butt end of the pen against the page. "Which of these people could've had the most interaction — and access — to Abi on a normal basis? Who is she most likely to talk to, text, and see after or outside of school?"

"Jasper is still my main pick," I say. "He saw her in class every day and left things in her locker. Look at what happened today; he's still going by her locker and dropping little things off. I saw him sneaking around the halls while I was in Spanish today."

When they both give me a confused look, it reminds me that I haven't told them about following Jasper yet. "Sorry, my bad," I say before immediately launching into finding him at Abi's locker, the woman who approached him, and the kiss to one of the photos.

Em stares at me when I'm done talking, blinks once, then puts a little star by his name. There's that heavy silence that fills the room once again, but I'm not sure if it's because we're all thinking of what to do now or they're trying to process what I'd said.

"As much as I don't want to say it, Mr. Clarke could be in the running." Em puffs her bottom lip out. Em likes English, so it makes sense that she wouldn't want it to be him.

"*Lo siento.*" My words cause her to roll her eyes while Maddi stares at me confused. "It means 'I'm sorry'."

To Maddi's defense, I don't think I've ever spoken Spanish in front of her before. Neither Abi nor Maddi know it, and Mom's never used it with them in the house.

"Anyway," I say, "Mr. Clarke is one of Abi's favorite teachers. They definitely spend time together. I don't know how much, but they used to talk about books outside of the readings, and sometimes she stayed after class so he could help with some of her essay work for her BCC application. Besides, if Mr. Perkins can be a suspect, so can Mr. Clarke."

Maddi gives me a thankful smile. It's obvious she's thinking back to our conversation the other day.

I told you; every person, every perspective... or I'm trying, at least.

"Jesse has math with Abi, but she loathes the dude. She mentioned how he's always a dick to her." I trace over some of the designs on the front of the journal with my index finger. "There's no way she'd talk to him for an assignment let alone spend time with him outside of school."

"And Tatum is so far up his own butt that he probably wouldn't notice if a thirty-foot Godzilla walked past." Em's words make Maddi laugh. After a few more moments processing what's on the page, Em draws in a deep breath and exhales it slowly. "So, are we going to fight Jasper tomorrow or what?"

"*Fight* him?" I've never seen Maddi's eyes go so wide so quickly. She looks like a baby deer.

"She's kidding," I say, "but I agree that we should talk to him. If we get there early enough, we can catch him in the courtyard before homeroom."

"I'm in. I'll be on standby in case he tries anything." Em holds up her fists.

"I stand by what I said: we call the cops if he admits it. We have a lot of evidence proving that Abi didn't just run away now. We have proof that someone was following her, that she might've been drugged, that whoever is behind the texts was manipulating the situation in some way. If he admits it, it's game over, isn't it? We hand them their entire case right then and there." Maddi looks between Em and me.

"The cops gave up on her, Maddi. They decided she wasn't worth looking into or finding. *We* made it this far. We owe it to her to see it through. Besides, anything they do will take a lot longer than us getting it done."

"I know, Hunter, but—"

I cut her off, "But nothing." I collect the laptop, journal, and phone into a pile again. "You were all for confronting him the other day. What happened to that? I'm not going to wait for some cop to get a warrant. By the time that happens, we might not see Abi again, and something worse than being kidnapped could happen to her." Is it harsh? Yes, but she needs to understand the gravity of the situation. Abi needs to be brought home. She's already been missing for two weeks, and the longer she's gone, the smaller the chances of us finding her safe — or alive — become.

Maddi narrows her eyes. "I *do* think we should confront him, but I think the cops should take it from there."

I don't verbally respond, but based on the clearing of Em's throat, anger is reading on my face. I try to remind myself it's not the time or place to argue — and especially not with Maddi.

"Let's just see what happens tomorrow," Em says, trying to diffuse the situation.

Maddi looks at Em in confusion. "A-are you serious? I thought you, of all people, would want to go to the police. That's what happens in all the detective shows. People follow the law, don't they?"

Her words cause Em to pause, clench her jaw, and take in another deep breath. It's a valid point, and while Em is the true crime enthusiast of the group, she trusts the cops even less than I do. They've screwed her over one too many times for her to immediately want their help.

There's an internal battle going on in her that's raging between the decision of handling this ourselves and playing detective or going to the police and risking what could happen. Em isn't stupid, I'm sure she knows that this can turn bad pretty quick, but like I've said before: the girl is stubborn.

"Think about it this way: we confront Jasper and see what he says. If we manage to get him to confess, there are two witnesses to it to add to the cop's case. It only helps them and makes it quicker to find Abi once we do turn things over, doesn't it?" Em nudges me with a wide smile to try and get me to lighten up. "Besides, you guys got to play detective. It's only fair that I get to too, right? We see what he says and go from there. Deal?"

Maddi sighs, obviously disliking the plan but knowing she isn't going to win a two-against-one battle. "Yeah, deal."

"Fine," I mumble.

Suspect List:
Jasper DeFoe
~~Jesse Barnum~~
~~Tatum Jones~~
Mr. Clarke
License place — _ <u>R</u> _ _ _ _

Twenty-One

Days since Abi's disappearance: 16

My sister can be overprotective, and when she thinks someone might try to hurt me — despite the fact that I can take care of myself — she convinces herself she needs to handle it. A great example of this is a situation from back in elementary school. A kid on the playground decided he wanted the swing before I was ready to get off of it, so he knocked me off and got on himself. Before I even had time to get off the ground, Em was right there with a right hook most adults would kill for. The kid ended up running toward the nurse's office with a bloody nose. I'm scrappy, but my sister is a pit bull.

Given that background, I do my best to make sure Em doesn't go into the situation with Jasper swinging — literally — but despite my best efforts, Em ends up going to school in "fight mode."

"Jasper!" she shouts in a horrendously chipper tone that's half an octave higher than normal. It immediately reminds me of Casey, causing yet another internal cringe. A few people in the courtyard glance her way. She's going to try to charm him into talking to us, I can already tell. "Jas, Jasper, *Jasperella*. How ya' doin', my guy?" The arm she loops around his shoulders pulls him close so he can't get away.

He tries anyway.

"Uhm, hi?" He glances toward her, then looks to the ground.

At least make eye contact. She's not going to bite you... well, maybe... but not hard... well...

"Hunter and I — you know my brother, Hunter." She points at me. I give Jasper an up-nod, but the smile I get back from him is weak and nervous. "Yeah, we wanna talk to ya for a second. Think we could do that?" Her arm pumps several small squeezes, jostling him against her. "Aah, of *course* it's okay! C'mon! Follow me." With her hand wrapping around his, I watch Em nearly drag the poor boy across the courtyard, into the main hallway, then to an empty classroom while I follow behind them.

I close the door behind me and glare at Jasper. The timid nature I've observed from him so far is nothing compared to right now. I can tell he'd rather be melting into the walls and disappearing than be anywhere near us.

Are you scared or are you trying to hide something?

In an attempt to keep his distance from Em and me, Jasper moves across the room before stopping near the teacher's desk at the front of the room. The way his eyes dart between us makes him resemble a cornered animal — nervous and unpredictable.

"Jasper... DeFoe, right?" I lean back against a desk in the front row and cross my arms.

He nods.

"And you're... Abi's science partner." It isn't a question, I'm confirming. Testing.

Jasper nods again, then glances in Em's direction.

Em, who's taken up residence leaning against the window and is using a knife cleverly disguised as a pen to clean her nails, doesn't bother looking up. "Keep starin' and I'll turn you into a past tense hashtag, buddy-boy."

She's letting me take the reins on things now that we're all together, which is probably for the best. We've perfected this dynamic: good cop, bad cop for lack of better phrasing. I'm the one that talks, the one that asks all the questions, and if someone doesn't cooperate, she, well, makes them.

Her quip is enough to make Jasper think I'm suddenly very interesting and look my way again. "Is she allowed to have that here?"

Em scoffs, rolls her eyes, and drops her hands to her sides. "It's a knife. You think I'm going to walk around our neighborhood without a little protection? And what are the teachers going to do? Pat me down?" she asks with a smirk. "I've got two more on me right now. Wanna find 'em?" She pushes away from the window to start walking toward him.

"Em," I say without so much as a glance her way. It's a subliminal warning. Jasper looks me in the eye finally, and my stare locks on him. On more than one occasion, Em has said it can be extremely uncomfortable to be on the other side of this particular stare. Apparently, I hardly blink and my eyes narrow. I wonder if it's similar to what Mr. Clarke gave me yesterday.

Maybe he was *studying me yesterday.*

"Have you ever called Abi?"

He shakes his head.

"Have you ever met her outside of school?"

He nods and shifts his weight from one hip to another with a glance at the door.

I clear my throat. "Have you ever taken her to get milkshakes?"

He shakes his head again, but this time his eyebrows press together.

Interesting.

"Have you ever heard of a place called McMullins?"

He pauses, thinks, then shakes his head again. "No. Look, I don't know what this is about, but I-I told Abi she was pretty, put a note in her locker once, and we studied a couple times at the library for tests, but that was it. Why are you asking me all these questions?"

I push off from the desk to walk toward him. The closer I get, the smaller he makes himself. I stop when I'm a half foot away, that bubbling anger rising to the surface again. Despite being taller than Abi, he's still shorter than me by almost three inches and, boy, does it make him uneasy. If I didn't know any better, I'd swear I could see the boy shaking. "Why were you at her locker yesterday?"

"How did you—"

I interrupt him to say, "Not what I asked." My earlier tone was flat and intense, but this one is low, intimidating. There's panic behind Jasper's expression, and the longer I study him, the more I see he's a scared little boy more than anything else.

This isn't someone who could overpower Abi even in a drugged up state. This isn't someone who's confident enough to kidnap someone, let alone send those texts.

The thought of being wrong deflates the anger and replaces it with defeat.

We're going to be back at square one after this unless something else comes up.

I hold my stare on him for another minute, then scoff and take a couple steps back.

"Jasper, breathe. I'm not going to hurt you. I don't really want to deal with the principal." My words don't comfort him, but at least he's not acting like a mouse trying to make itself invisible to a hungry cat anymore. I do my best to bring a somewhat friendly sounding tone to my words. "We were looking into Abi's disappearance, and your name came up. Gotta follow the leads, right? But, just to be clear, you only hung out with Abi at the library, nowhere else, and you've never been to a diner called McMullins."

Jasper draws in a deep breath, nodding. I can see the muscles in his jaw protruding with how hard he's clenching it shut.

"Awesome. Thanks for your time." I nod toward the door and watch him scramble out of the room. Once he's gone, my shoulders slouch.

What are we supposed to do now?

When I turn to look at her, Em is already seated in the teacher's chair with her legs propped up on the desk. "So, you think he did it?"

I make my way over to the desk I'd been leaning on before and sit down in the chair to face her like a pupil to their teacher. "Before this talk? Yeah, one hundred percent. Now?" I let the silence answer the question.

She scoffs and lets her head fall back against the chair as she twists herself a few inches back and forth. "That boy is more spineless than a jellyfish. Did you see the way he cowered when you walked toward him? I thought he was going to wet himself." She giggles, obviously taking amusement in the visual.

I run over every piece of evidence we've found, every event I've learned about, everything Casey told us. "You think he could be putting on a show? Those texts... they went from room temperature, to hot, to cold, to broiling, and back again. What if he's saying those things to us and acting this way so no one suspects him?" Even I know it's a long shot.

Em's eyes lock on the ceiling while thinking. "I mean, I could go beat him up a little for ya. These hands—" she balls her fists and holds them to the ceiling. "—They're rated E for Everyone!" With a one-two jab into the air toward whatever she's been staring at, she laughs. I find it's a sound I need, and it brings a smile.

"No need to scare the kid any more than he already is. We'll just keep an eye on him for now." I shrug while staring at the initials carved into the desk in front of me. *R &J* with a heart around it.

"Should we tell Maddi?" She kicks her legs off the desk and leans forward to look at me. "She seemed really against us doing all of this yesterday."

"She wasn't against *this*, but she wants to follow the rules, and I get it. Abi probably would want to do the same thing, but what if the cops can't find her the way we can? Or it takes too long? Not to get all criminal, but it's faster to break into someone's house." Sure, it's morally corrupt to break into someone's house, but it's also morally corrupt to kidnap and hold someone hostage. Two wrongs don't make a right, but is a wrong really wrong when it has good intentions? "You think the cops would drop the B-and-E charges if we save someone's life?"

"This isn't a show, Hunter, we need to play it safe where we can. There's no script. We don't know this will all have a happy ending. This is real life, and I don't want to lose you because you're being a stubborn, tough guy. If we manage to find whoever did this and we go up against them..." It's strange to see worry from her. She's always the hype person, my fearless co-pilot, so when she gets nervous, it's time for me to pay attention.

"Em." I stand and walk over to the teacher's desk, then lean forward to press my palms on the wood and look at her. "I *need* to do this, and I need your support with it."

She chews on the inside of her bottom lip. I watch that internal battle rage once again, but ultimately, she nods and there's a sense of relief that washes over me. "Alright, fine. Let's figure out who did this and bring her home."

TWENTY-TWO

— • —

Days since Abi's disappearance: 18

A few break-ins happen every month. It's pretty common on this side of town, but it's usually people stealing TVs or stereos or something else of value that can be sold. What doesn't usually happen is having your house broken into and only one specific room being ransacked.

"EMERALD!" My room is a mess, torn to absolute shreds. The mattress is flipped, drawers are opened, the closet door is ajar with clothes and shoes thrown across the floor. "Em! Get in here!" I don't know what to do, I don't want to move. Someone came into our house. Someone has been in *my room*. Why? What could they possibly....

Oh no.

Fear floods me so fast an icy chill sends a shock from deep in my gut. I dart toward the other side of my bed and drop to my knees during a skid across the floor. A few things are pushed aside so I can look under the frame, and... nothing.

No—no—no... no. This can't be happening.

I fling things behind me, push items away and out from under my bed. The faster my breathing becomes, the faster the fear turns to panic. Where is everything? Where's the laptop and journal and phone and notebook?

It's got to be here somewhere. I'm missing it. I have to be.

"What? What is it?" Her words are breathless from running up the stairs. "Oh my... for Christ's sake. Hunter, what ha—who?"

At least it's not just me who can't form sentences.

I push myself back to sit while a hand runs up my forehead and down the back of my head. It's times like this that I wish I let my hair grow more than a few inches. Typically, I keep it pretty short, not quite a buzz cut but not long enough to spike either. But, man, does ripping some hair out right at the root sounds great right about now.

"They took it, Em. All of it." How could I be so stupid to leave everything in such an easy place?

I should've hidden it better. I should've done something to protect it.

I scoff, then kick a shoe away from me and turn to sit with my back against the bed frame. "Someone must've found out what we were doing, found out I was holding things, and broke in."

Em settles herself next to me but doesn't say anything right away. "We'll figure it out, okay? We will." She's trying to be encouraging, and it's sweet of her, but I'm responsible for this. I should've hidden the evidence in a better spot, I gave information out in a public space knowing it was risky, and I mentioned the evidence being at our place. It was all me.

"Them taking things...." Her words trail off, but she doesn't need to finish the sentence. I understand. She's thinking this means we're close; this means we had what we needed to find out who took Abi. Only problem is it also means whoever took Abi is someone that's been around us recently, someone that would've heard us talking.

It's someone at school.

The prickle at the corner of my eyes comes back accompanying a tidal wave of desire to be comforted by Abi, and my mind complies by playing memories of Abi hugging me and whispering, "It's going to be okay. We'll get through it together."

I'm so sorry, Abi...

"Yeah. I know, Em," I say before dropping my head back. I stare at the ceiling and try to push passed the self-loathing.

Feeling sorry for yourself isn't going to fix any of this, Hunter. Get it together. You told Maddi to suck it up. It's your turn.

"It was Jasper. It can't be a coincidence that the day after we decide to talk to him this happens. It can't." I pull out my phone to text Maddi but stop and let my hands fall into my lap.

"What if she was right?" I ask. "What if we should've gone to the cops? We should've taken everything we'd collected and told them "here you go." If this sicko has everything, there's no evidence. No way to link anyone to the crime. Nothing. There's Casey, but that won't go anywhere if there's nothing linking whoever was at the diner to this stalker. There's not even evidence of the stalker because her laptop and phone are gone."

I'm spiraling. I want to make it stop, but I can't. Despite my internal demands to be strong, my head is betraying me. It's cruel and intrusive and venomous. The world is caving in, like I'm in a tiny box and can't find my way out.

Pull yourself together, Greene! Abi needs you!

"Hunter, stop, it'll be okay. I promise." Em's words come through in Abi's voice, but the tone is anything but comforting. Sharp, piercing. She pulls me into a hug and normally I'd pull away and make some playful, snide comment about her getting soft, but I can't bring myself to. Instead, I close my eyes and try to calm my mind amongst her comfort.

None of this feels fair or right or just. How could we work so hard and figure out so much only to be sent back to *true* square one so quick? Pulling back from her, I look back to my phone.

ME: EVERYTHING'S GONE.

MADELEINE: WHAT DO YOU MEAN?

ME: SOMEONE BROKE IN. TOOK EVERYTHING.

MADELEINE: ALL OF IT?!

ME: YUP.

ME: That's what I walked into.
MADELEINE: Jesus.
MADELEINE: What do we do?
ME: What CAN we do?

I stare at the screen after sending the last text, sigh, and continue typing. It sounds snappy, and that's not what I want to give her.
Reign it in, Greene. Stop being a dick.

ME: I guess we wait? This D person has all the evidence we've collected. We can't do anything now. We have your text about the milkshakes, but without Abi's phone or laptop, there's no way to prove that she had a stalker or someone following her, let alone who took her to the diner.
MADELEINE: We'll figure something out.

At least she doesn't say "I told you so," however, if there's one thing I hate more than an "I told you so," it's "we'll figure something out" or "have some faith."

Faith gives you comfort when you're trying to come to terms with a death. Faith allows you to keep going when life feels pointless. Faith doesn't get people out of bad situations like this. Faith doesn't miraculously give you evidence that someone stole. My mind replays Em's warning: "This isn't a show, Hunter, we need to play it safe where we can."

I should've listened.

"When would he have had time to do this?" Em's words pull me from my thoughts.

"What do you mean?"

"Jasper. When would he have time to sneak out of school, search the room, grab the evidence, stash it somewhere, and get back to school before anyone noticed? He didn't do it after school, we came straight home."

She has a point.

"Do you—" My jaw clenches as a new thought swirls in my head. "Do you think he has an accomplice?"

She pauses then says, "It's possible. Either that, or someone overheard us."

That's obvious. They wouldn't know otherwise.

"We've been so careful though. The only time we've mentioned it out of this room is the other day in Mr. Clarke's class, but I tried to be as vague as possible." I turn to look at her properly. She's still wearing that worried expression, but her eyes tell me she's shifting into "fixer mode." She's trying to build a plan. She's trying to find a way to make this all feel less hopeless.

"You can be as vague as you want, but if someone is involved or has a guilty conscience, they're going to connect the dots." Again, she has a point.

I replay the events of the last few days in my head.

"Jasper was sitting a couple seats behind you in English that day. He could've heard what we were talking about, pieced it together somehow, and made a plan. If he does have a partner, he could've tipped them off." My eyes focus on something behind Em while my mind wanders and replays everything. The more I think about Jasper being involved, the angrier I become. He did this. He took her, and now there's no way to prove it.

He can't get away with this. I won't let him.

"Yeah, but even you didn't think he could've done it after we confronted him. I really don't know if that whole thing was an a—"

"Yeah, but I also saw him kiss a picture taped to her locker, Em." My tone, alone, makes her sit up straighter. I've moved passed the upset and anger, and into determined rage. "Clearly, he was putting on an act if this happened. We confronted him about things, he put on the *good boy* act so we'd discount him, and he tipped off whoever he's working with or figured out how to slip away from school."

Em opens her mouth to speak, but I continue before she can.

"I've played it safe this long. I've done things the right way, compiled evidence, and look where it got us. I'm done playing nice. I'm done with the kid gloves. I'm finding her and I'm bringing her home no matter who I need to rough up."

TWENTY-THREE

Days since Abi's disappearance: 19

It isn't a simple or easy plan, but it's a plan that can give us solid answers. With all of the evidence taken, the search for Abi is at a standstill, leaving us one thing to do: find it. If we find it, we find *D*, we find Abi. It doesn't take too much to convince Em to make our starting place Jasper. Maddi, on the other hand, is an entirely different story.

"It'll be fine." Em makes the whole thing sound so easy. We've gone over the plan with Maddi several times, but each time she tries to poke a hole in why something won't work. If we ask her to sit with him at lunch to keep an eye on him, she tells us his friends will think it's weird. If we ask her to distract him in the hall in between classes, she talks about how she has perfect attendance and doesn't want to ruin her chances at honor roll.

Sometimes it feels like this whole thing would be easier without you.

Sure, we wouldn't be on this adventure if it wasn't for her tip-off about the text message, but I'm finding a lot of frustration when she does nothing other than shoot down plan after plan.

"I don't know...."

"Look," I say, "all you gotta do is talk to him for, what, five minutes. Tops. We're just going to look through a few things in his locker and get out of there, but we can't do that if there's a risk of him seeing us."

"Exactly, we need to see if he's hiding anything in there," Em says.

Maddi looks between the two of us, hands twisting at the strap of her backpack slowly. "Okay...." It sounds more like a question than an answer.

"Great!" Em's overenthusiastic tone makes Maddi flinch. "He's right there, have fun!" She pushes Maddi toward the science classroom, then grabs my hand and nearly drags me in the opposite direction. "We need to move fast," she says.

"I'm aware." I rip my hand from hers then match her pace.

Jasper's locker is halfway down the next hallway and around the corner. It won't be hard for him to get to us quickly if he figures out what we're doing, but hopefully Maddi can keep him busy long enough.

"You have the combination?" I ask.

"Does a porcupine shoot its quills as a defense mechanism to predators?"

"...Sometimes I wonder how we're related, but, also, no. It doesn't."

"Yeah, same." She glances over her shoulder with a smirk. "And maybe it doesn't, but it still uses it's quills to defend itself."

Acquiring Jasper's locker combination was a fun little cocktail of flirtation and distraction — Em's favorite. Michael Rodriguez is the student volunteer that works in the front office during his free hour, and one of Em's biggest fans. He's fully aware of her relationship with Cai, but when you're lovesick, you're lovesick, I guess. After a couple of days of stopping in to talk to him and buttering him up, she was able to bat her eyelashes and promise him a couple sweet nothings in exchange for the code to Jasper's locker.

"So, you're telling me you promised him a date to see how you two 'fit' and he gave this up?"

"Essentially, but I had to be very convincing," she says while glancing over her shoulder again.

"How will Cai feel about this?"

"I get a free meal and he gets leftovers." I can hear the smirk in her words as she continues working on the lock. "Maybe you two can have a 'bro night' or something."

It has been a while since just the two of us hung out.

"Aaaand, we're in." She hands me the lock and opens the door.

The lockers are pretty small. You can't hold much in there unless you organize it pretty well. Jasper's locker? It is an utter disaster. His locker makes Em's room look like mine. It has old food wrappers, crumpled papers, a few binders that are in such disarray we can't make out what class they're for, and stickers covering nearly every inch of the metal on the inside. I pull out a stack of papers and glance through them. There are old science tests, a couple of low-score English papers, and a schedule from last spring.

Man, this kid is a pack rat.

"Are... are you kidding me?" I ask and hand Em some of the papers.

"Dude, this is...."

"Yeah. Tell me about it."

We do our best to wade through the different papers and items inside the locker, but eventually give up and determine there's nothing of use to us in there. It's disappointing, and it leaves us with only one option from here, but at least we don't need to wonder anymore.

"So, it looks like we're breaking into the DeFoe house, huh?" There's a sparkle in Em's eye that makes me shake my head. My sister is a convict waiting to happen.

"You really shouldn't be so excited to break into things," I say.

"Well, what's the fun in life if you can't break a few laws, *Hunter*?" Her head bobs from side to side with the attitude-fueled tone while her arms cross.

I give an amused scoff in response, then roll my eyes and hand her the lock. "Let's lock this thing back up and get out of here. I want to go wash my hands or... organize my own locker."

The longer I think about the fact that we didn't find anything, the more that anger starts to churn again. If it's not here, that means he's keeping everything somewhere else. We need to get to his house, we need to search his room. Maybe he has a shed or a basement or an attic that he keeps things — or people — in.

We're turning to leave when I hear Em draw in a deep breath through her nose and release a frustrated growl. Part of me is afraid to look at what she's focusing on. Has someone been watching us this whole time? Did someone see what we were doing? Maybe the person who did this caught us searching and is trying to confront us now. When I finally turn, I'm halfway through the movement before I see *him*.

"What are you doing?" The timid tone is evident, and there's what looks like a strange combination of fear and fury in his eyes. Did he have something to hide in there that we missed? Now I want to go back for a second look.

"Nothing," Em says and flashes him a charming, albeit sarcastic, smile.

"Yeah, people don't just go searching through a locker that's not theirs for no reason. How did you get in anyway?"

Someone's confrontational today. Careful, buddy boy, too much attitude and Em will swing.

"First of all—"

"We know it was you," I say while simultaneously cutting Em's words off and stepping in front of her. I can feel her shift behind me, but I follow the movement to keep her from facing him again. I'm handling this, not her, and I need her out of the way. The longer I stare at Jasper, the more I want to yell, the more I want to scream, the tighter my fist balls.

You did this. I know you did. You did this, you took her, now tell us where she is.

"Wh-what are you talking about?" With me now at the forefront of the confrontation, it seems that mouse-like nature is creeping back up. Is he only afraid of me? Why? Because I'm taller than him? Em hits harder than I do on a good day, she can do more damage than me if she really wants to.

"I'm talking about Abi — I know you remember her. I've seen you moping around the halls, pretending to be *so sad* that she's gone, but it was you. You were the one who took her." I take a step forward and he immediately flinches like I've given him a physical threat.

You're pathetic.

"N-no! I didn—"

"I'm sick of you lying to me!" Something in me snaps, and I no longer care about composure. Screw being proper; screw the rules; screw all of this! Abi deserves to be home, happy, with her family. With *me.*

I uncurl my fist enough to grab the front of Jasper's shirt and shift us both to the side. His back hits the lockers so hard the metal *bang* echoes off the walls and causes a pause in the sounds around us. He's already shaking, but all sympathy for him is gone. He should've thought about these things when he took her. He should've thought about what would happen when I found out before he decided to be a selfish prick and collect someone like they were a prized item to be held in a case.

People aren't objects. You don't collect them!

"Don't. Lie. To. Me." My words are pointed, staccato. I want it to be very clear to him that it's in his best interest to be both direct and honest. "I'm having a very bad week, DeFoe, and I'm itching to take it out on someone." My words hiss through teeth that have clenched themselves so hard my jaw hurts. The blood rushing in my ears drowns out the sounds around us until someone touches my shoulder.

"Hunter," Maddi says. I can hear her, but it's so far off, it's easy to ignore.

"Where is she?!" My yell makes Jasper flinch again and shrink into his shoulders.

"I don't know! I swear! Please, I didn't do anything."

My fist slams into the locker door next to his head, causing a dent in the metal. The pain coursing through my hand forces my mind to focus on that and some of my anger ebbs away.

"Hunter!" Maddi's voice is closer this time, causing me to whip around and look at her.

"And *you!* We told you to distract him. We told you that he needed to stay busy, so this didn't happen. You couldn't do one simple thing? What would've happened if we found something, and he walked in on us?" My steps toward her are slow, menacing.

"D-did y—"

"It doesn't matter now, does it? You couldn't even follow one simple instruction. Seriously, Maddi. It's not that hard to talk to someone." My words are acidic. I can see the impact they're having on her. I'm watching her crumble and break, but I can't stop the words from leaving me. I can't stop the thoughts before they come out. "I needed one thing from you. ONE."

"I'm sorry, I am. I was chasing after him so he wou— it's not my fault that he—" Behind her eyes are millions of thoughts she can't form words for, but I can see them. I can read them plainly on her features. She was going after him when he found us. She was trying to do what we asked. Maddi is doing the best she can.

You're taking your bottled-up anger out on her. You're focusing on one thing — Jasper being the culprit — and it's clouding your judgment. Breathe. You need to breathe.

I don't want to breathe, though. I want to hit something. I want to fight. I want this all to be over so life can go back to normal. This is our senior year, it's supposed to be smooth sailing from here on out until we start college in the fall. This is supposed to be our relaxation year, not the "my girlfriend has been missing for almost a month and we still have no idea where she is" year.

"You're sorry," I say with a scoff. "Okay."

"I am! I—"

"I really don't care right now, *Madeleine*." My tone is a little more level than the last, but the emphasis on her name still brings that acidic nature back.

"Mr. Greene!" The voice bellows and echoes against the halls like a shockwave.

Principal Sanchez.

"What?" My voice barks back just as loud as his. When I turn to look at him, his arms are crossed and the pencil-thin mustache lining his upper lip is curled at a strange angle distorting his snarl. He doesn't like being talked back to, and there hasn't been a time we encountered each other that I've rolled over and taken whatever he has to say without something to say back.

"My office. Now." He doesn't wait for a response.

TWENTY-FOUR

Days since Abi's disappearance: 20

The display in the hallway gets me a one-week suspension for "bullying and attempting to incite violence with a fellow student." It probably would've only been three days had I not promptly corrected Principal Sanchez by saying "you can't incite violence with someone incapable of handling confrontation." As true as the words are, giving attitude to a school official always causes more issues and earns you another label as "insubordinate."

Because I'm sent home early, Mom decided to take a half day at work. I already know there's no way she's going to get a call like that and not be at the house waiting to rip me a new one. It takes a long conversation and many promises that it won't happen again before she finally lets me go back to my room with a punishment of a two-week grounding.

According to Em, she made the decision to use the rest of her day at school to formulate a new plan to follow Jasper home. The most difficult thing about finding out where Jasper lives is making sure he doesn't leave school too quickly. After the attempt Octavia interrupted, Em and I tried to follow him on two more occasions, but he was able to evade us both times. I don't know if he knows we're on to him and he's purposely avoiding us or if he hates school so much he rushes out as fast as possible every day like someone is trying to chase him down. Most kids stop and talk to their friends after school or wait for the big rush of everyone trying to leave the parking lot to thin out, but not Jasper. Maybe that's how life works for people who don't have a big social circle. Em ended up having to sprint to the car to leave in time to follow him. Luckily, she only took down his address and didn't go inside or confront him. One thing I don't want is her impulsive, confrontational side taking over when I'm not there.

He had someone help him. That's how he got the stuff from the house.

The next morning — after mom leaves, and we're sure she isn't coming back for anything — Em and I drive to the DeFoe house and wait. The easiest and safest time to get in and search the place is when everyone's gone. When does that typically happen? During a weekday. It means Em has to skip school and I have to break my grounding, but it's in the name of finding Abi and the evidence, so I give it a pass. Hopefully Mom will too. Scratch that. We'll just have to make sure Mom doesn't find out.

———

After pulling up to the DeFoe residence, I grab my phone.

ME: JUST ARRIVED AT JASPER'S. WILL TEXT WHEN WE'RE LEAVING.
MADELEINE: OKAY. DON'T GET CAUGHT.
ME: THAT'S THE NAME OF THE GAME.

"This is like a stakeout," Em says while bouncing in her seat when I look up from the screen.

"You're way too excited about this."

"Oh, *c'mooonn*, you don't think this is exciting?" The giggle that erupts from her makes my ears hurt. It's obvious she's excited to finally be fully involved in all of this, but sometimes I worry about the amount of excitement she has about these situations. One day, I'm going to end up bailing her out of jail because she took some rich kid's car for a joy ride or broke into a house for the adrenaline rush. She adds, "We could be catching a kidnapper!"

"Yeah, that's kind of the point of all of this."

She slaps my arm and huffs. "I don't need your sass right now. You're not going to bring down my moment."

Your moment? I thought we were supposed to be catching a kidnapper.

"So, what happens if it is him? He's obviously not going to keep her here. It's too risky with his family. You think he has somewhere to keep her? Family's secondary house or cabin? Old mill? A well of some kind?"

Em turns toward me slowly. "Hunter Greene, I swear if you start talking about making her put lotion on her skin..."

I mimic the way she turns and say, "What? Are you going to make me use the hose again?"

She tries to hide a smile but ends up erupting into a snort. There are very few people I can joke with about this kind of stuff. It's not an obscure type of reference — not if you're a horror or psychological thriller fan — but there's a finesse to dark humor that not a lot of people have or understand. Em, thankfully, appreciates and enjoys not-so-socially-appropriate jokes.

"OH!" She slaps my arm again and points to the house. "They're leaving, look."

I slap her back but look at the house as instructed. A man, woman, and younger boy exit the house and head toward a blue SUV while Jasper locks the front door. The kid is yelling about wanting to get a treat before going to school, and although the woman's response is inaudible, her body language tells me she's simultaneously telling him no and that he needs to quiet down.

Once they're gone and the car is far enough down the street that we're sure they won't spot us, Em and I are out of the car and jogging toward the house.

"I'll go around and check the back," she says before disappearing. Throughout her years of doing hoodlum activities, she's come to learn that the majority of people will lock their doors but forget about their windows.

While waiting, I turn and look around the street, partially to make sure we weren't being watched and partially to know what is around.

You're being paranoid.

The door opens behind me and an accomplished sigh leaves Em. "Ready?"

"As ever," I say and head inside.

Much like Maddi and Abi, it seems Jasper shares the conjoining bathroom with his brother. We originally go into the youngest DeFoe's room and find it's covered in different types of dinosaurs and race cars and rocket ship models. The kid is eclectic, I'll give him that much. After a quick walk through the bathroom, we emerge into a room that's more reminiscent of the explosion of a trash can and dresser than bedroom. Clothes litter the floor, trash is scattered around, and there's a smell that I can only describe as old gym socks and mildew.

"Is... this what other guy's rooms look like? I've been in Cai's room, it does not look like this." I try to not sound disgusted, but my skin is already crawling. I'm not a germaphobe, but I believe there's a level of cleanliness everyone should keep for a comfortable environment. A sentiment Jasper clearly doesn't share with me.

"I clean Cai's room a lot," Em says, "and normally rooms aren't *this* bad, but, yes. Most teenage boys don't organize their room like you."

I can't help the shudder that goes through me. Despite knowing my nose will hate me for it, I take in a deep breath and exhale a slow, heavy sigh. "Alright, well, I guess we need to get to it."

We spend the next thirty minutes searching the room. Em searches under the bed, the nightstand, the desk, and bookshelves while I take the closet, wall shelves, and floor. By the time we've searched everything, all I want to do is shower and burn my clothes. After finding a clear section of wall that doesn't look overly contaminated, I lean against it and sigh as my eyes focus on a sock in front of me.

"Nothing, seriously. This sucks."

"If you want to look on the bright side, we learned that he doesn't have any of it?" Em says.

I'm not in the mood for optimism right now.

I feel defeated in a way I haven't felt before — even after questioning Jasper. This is lower, deeper. It feels like we aren't getting anywhere with our investigation, and we *won't* be getting anywhere. "Let's just head home," I say finally and nod toward the door leading to the hallway while texting Maddi.

ME: HEADING OUT. DIDN'T FIND ANYTHING. COME OVER AFTER DINNER TO DISCUSS THINGS?

MADELEINE: OKAY, SEE YOU TONIGHT.

"We'll figure it out," she says.

"That's what everyone keeps saying."

Once Maddi makes it to the house, and after filling her in on everything we found — or didn't find — in Jasper's locker and room, the three of us sit in silence. Again. Em has decided her fingernails are in need of attention, and Maddi looks as if someone just told her a cat got run over.

"So, what are we supposed to do?" Maddi asks.

Em and I both shrug.

"That's not an answer. You two want to, what, give up?"

"No one's saying that," I say, "but there's also no other leads right now. I've scoured every piece of that laptop and every word of the journal. We didn't have the phone long enough to look through everything. Whoever this is, they knew what we had —

or at least that we had things to start finding her — and…" I let my words fade out. "Forget it."

Maddi's judging my decision, it's obvious. She wants us to take action, but what action is there to take? All of our progress is gone. We have no evidence, no proof, and nowhere to go from here.

"There has to be something."

"Like what?" Em asks.

"I don't know. *Something.*" Maddi turns to me. "You're the one who said we could do this, and now you're giving up? That's not the Hunter I know. You were the one who convinced me this is worth it, and we can find her. You were the one who did all the legwork. You were the one who made this such a big mission. The Hunter I know doesn't just give up. He doesn't let anyone stop him from doing something, and when they try, he uses spite to prove them wrong. And you." She turns to Em. "You're feisty and aren't afraid to ruffle some feathers to get what you want. Didn't you once go out with a kid for two weeks so he'd get you premiere tickets to some movie downtown?"

"It was a good movie," Em huffs and rolls her eyes.

I try to keep a straight face, but the memory makes me give a half-cocked smirk.

"Sorry," I say as the smirk fades. When I look at Maddi, the look of anger and disappointment on her features causes a sigh.

"Well, fine." She stands from the bed. "If you want to sit here and be all 'woe is me' about this, go ahead, but don't call me when something else happens. I tried to help. I tried to motivate you. I tried to keep your spirits up."

I want to tell her it was a great pick-me-up speech and that I understand the sentiment, but the way she turns her tone to belittle me just causes the bubbling anger again, and before I can stop it, everything boils over.

"You're the one who didn't want us to do all of this anyway," I snap. "You wanted us to go to the cops immediately, and now you want to sit on a high horse about how we should keep going?

What about evidence? Huh? Tell me, *Madeleine,* what should we do with no leads and nothing to go off of? Do you know where she's being hidden or who has her? Do you have any idea who took her and why and how to find them? Because we can't just go to the cops without proof."

The more I rant, the louder my voice gets until I see Maddi shutting down like she does with her father. A new wave of guilt hits me, and I immediately regret every word.

Crap...

"Screw you, *Hunter.*" The way she says my name is venomous. She pauses, glaring at me with a look that would kill if it could. "You know what, you're right. I didn't want to do this, but I only didn't want to after *you* decided we shouldn't go to the cops. I knew it was a bad idea to wait. I wanted to follow what felt right. We found evidence, we had so much, and if you would've just *listened to me* then maybe my sister would be home right now." She narrows her eyes. "They failed *you* when they didn't find who killed your dad, that doesn't mean they'll fail *me* too. You're so hell bent on being the hero and fixating on the fact that *you* have to save her that you stopped listening and did whatever you wanted. If we'd gone to the cops when we found that phone number, they could've traced it. They could've looked into things from there. We had leads, and so much evidence, but it just wasn't enough for you. *You* caused this." The second she's done talking, she leaves.

The words are a punch to the gut. She's blaming me? She's blaming me for someone breaking into our house because I didn't want to go to the cops? How dare she. Doesn't she understand it makes no sense to trust them? Doesn't she understand that they've been nothing but sloppy with their side of things? And to bring my dad into this?

That was a low blow.

Yeah, the cops failed my family, and that's a big part of why I don't trust them, but they've messed up on other things too. Did she forget that they gave up on Abi less than a week after she went missing? Did she forget that they'd deemed her just another runaway and said she'd be back? Did she forget that they *already* failed her? I can't be all wrong simply because I want to make sure we have everything so Abi can be found and the guy will go away for good... could I?

Maybe she's right.

I immediately move to get up, but Em's hand on my leg stops me.

"Leave it. Let her go."

TWENTY-FIVE

Days since Abi's disappearance: 24

"Hunter, get up," Em says and yanks the comforter from me to toss it to the floor.

She's learned that if it's left on the bed, I'm going to pull it back over my head and not get up. I stopped caring about getting up or doing much of anything a couple of days ago. After the blowup with Maddi, it became hard to shake the lingering depression. I feel like an idiot for letting my anger take hold and spewing so many things at her, but I feel even worse the more I think about *her* words. The day the evidence was taken, I felt it was all my fault, but it felt like my fault because I didn't hide things well enough. However, I didn't want to listen to her when she suggested going to the cops, I wanted to solve every piece of the puzzle before trusting anyone else with what we had. I was fixated and in my own head — something Em tells me *not* to do, something Maddi warned me about too — and look at where it got us. The evidence was taken because I didn't hide things well enough. I didn't hide things well enough and wasn't secretive enough with things resulting in the evidence being taken. That never would've happened if I wasn't so dead set on solving this before going to the cops.

"Leave me alone," I pull the pillow over my head, and Em rips that off too without a word. "Emerald! Seriously." I turn my upper body in her direction with a pointed look before falling back on the bed to stare at the wall.

"Hunter, *seriously.*" She's trying — and failing — to hold back annoyance. I'm being stubborn.

How does it feel to not be listened to?

There's another minute or two of silence before she sits on the bed and lets out a heavy sigh. She places one of her hands on my back. It's soft and gentle. She's worried about me, and I appreciate her for it, but there isn't much to be done. I'm accepting the fact that I made the biggest mistake in all of this. I'm admitting, even if it's just to myself, that *I* am the reason we won't see Abi again. I'm mourning the inevitable loss of my girlfriend and the life we expected to have together, all because I acted out of ego and irrationality.

Just leave me to process in peace. I just want to be alone.

The thought triggers that conversation with Mr. Jenkins, but I'm hardly in a place to care about being emotionally vulnerable. It's not like anyone understands anyway. Why bring it up?

"Em, why does it matter?" I turn my head to her side of the bed but don't look at her. I stare ahead, not focusing on anything in particular.

"Because it's Halloween tomorrow, and we always do spooky things together." There's a pout in her words by the sound of them. "I figure if we can get you up and out of bed today, it'll be easier tomorrow. We'll go frighten some kids and collect candy and come home to watch scary movies. It's tradition."

"I really don't want to go out this year. It won't feel the same or right to go out and celebrate right now. You and Cai can do that stuff without me."

"Hunter Mateo Greene, I did not just hear you say that. I am not going out on Halloween without you. Are you kidding me? Especially when—" she leans forward and pinches my cheek while talking in a horrid baby voice, "—you're so down in the dumps."

I immediately push her off the bed, causing a hard thud as she hits the floor. I expect to hear an angered retort or a curse, but she laughs instead.

"Get out of here." I want to be angry with her, but even the words betray my efforts.

"Have you been studying for finals? Have you been doing *anything* from your normal, OCD riddled routine?" She sits upright and crosses her legs with her hands in her lap. "They're coming up in a few weeks."

"Ugh. Don't remind me." I lift my head before dragging myself into a seated position that mirrors hers. "I haven't done any studying in weeks."

"Yeah, because you became obsessed with finding Abi. I know things are hard right now, but whether Abi comes home or not, you know she wouldn't want you to throw away everything because of something like this — especially not because of her. She'd want you to keep pushing forward. I gave you your time to mope, now you need to get back up and moving." Em walks to my desk. "Where are all those test and homework papers?"

I gesture to the drawer, and she pulls out a stack of mismatched papers before coming back to sit on the bed.

"Why don't we study together tonight. We'll get your brain moving, get that noggin of yours in a better place, and then tomorrow we'll take things as it comes, okay? If we don't go out, we can order in and have Cai come over. We'll watch old black-and-white movies and try to make the best of things."

She's trying to make me feel included, but it's only making me feel like a third wheel. The four of us have always been a unit. If we were out, we were all out together. Double dates, random trips to the movies or local mall so the girls can window shop and try on things they know they'll never buy. Things changed a little when Cai went off to college last year, but when he's in town, the four of us are what makes our group. Not three.

The memories are painful to think about now. She should be out there with Cai having fun, dressed up in whatever little goth outfit and platform shoes she's chosen for the night. Cai, no doubt, will be in some sort of getup to match Em's. The two are a match made in weird, and I love that for them, but just the thought of being around them without Abi is torturous. They don't need me bringing down their fun.

"It's okay. I really don't want to dampen your plans."

Em picks up a pillow and whacks me with it, sending a few papers flying off the bed. "You're not dampening plans. I suggested them, didn't I? That means I want to do them *with you*. Cai doesn't care what we do. He was telling me the other day he misses his best friend and we should all have a night together soon." After setting the pillow down, she leans forward and scoops up some of the papers. Her pause in a hunched position makes me look at her.

"Hunter..." She pulls out the piece of ripped stationery from the pile while setting the test papers haphazardly on the bed. She glances at me, then back down at the item in her hand. Her expression is worried again, but I can't place why. "Is this what you guys were talking about when you first looked at the journal? That weird note that didn't make any sense?" She turns the paper so I can see it. The scratchy writing with random numbers and letters stares back at me, taunting me. It reminds me of what I've failed at and the lack of information we still have.

"Yeah, it must've gotten mixed up in the papers when everything fell off the bed that day. We couldn't figure out what it meant though, remember? Just toss it."

"No... I've seen this before!" An epiphany is hitting her, but all I can focus on is how dark her expression has become. "Oh god... you were right."

"What are you talking about?" I ask, annoyed.

"The stationery!" She turns it to show me again as if I'm supposed to understand. Those stupid black crows mock me this time, daring me to figure out where they came from and what the writing means. "Remember when Mr. Clarke had me take that note to the office?"

"Yeah. So wh—" I stop. "No... *No.*"

"There's the lightbulb! It was *this* stationery! This came from Mr. Clarke's desk. It had to have. I remember it because the crows remind me of that Edgar Allan Poe poem, *The Raven*."

Of course, it did.

Her stare forward is distant and almost lifeless. For once, I can't tell what she's thinking, but it's clear a mix of emotions are raging through her. "If *this* is one of those notes that was left in her locker, that means Mr. Clarke was on the other end of all those calls and texts. It means Mr. Clarke is *D*."

TWENTY-SIX

Days since Abi's disappearance: 24
My stomach drops and a chill hits my spine so hard, that ice bath feeling returns. This isn't real. This isn't happening. We didn't find our English teacher's stationery tucked inside my girlfriend's journal. Until now, the world kept feeling like like it was closing in on me, but now it feels like it's slipping away.

There's no way. It wasn't him. It doesn't make sense. He's... He's not dangerous, is he? Is he really the one behind all of this? The switch from sweet to possessive and sweet again?

Images flash through my mind back-to-back: Mr. Clarke at the café the day Maddi and I met, clearing his throat and interrupting us. The images immediately shift to Abi and Mr. Clarke at the diner; dragging her back to the car after drugging her; tying her up somewhere.

Why would Mr. Clarke leave notes for Abi? *Was* this one of the notes left in her locker? Even better question: Why does Abi have a phone number for him that isn't his normal number? Why does she have his phone number at all? My heart starts racing and that tightness in my chest I thought I'd gotten rid of comes back tenfold. I stare at Em, afraid that if I look anywhere else, I might yell, scream, or hit something.

It was Mr. Clarke? Was he the one who picked her up? The one texting her? The one that did all of this?

It all feels so surreal.

"He's a teacher." The words nearly rip through me. That all-too-familiar churning in my stomach starts again causing me to make a mental calculation on how many steps it will take me to get off the bed and into the bathroom before whatever is still in my stomach comes up. "They're supposed to protect us." How could he do this? *Why* would he do this? "I've seen him on his phone in class, and *D*'s number is disconnected."

"It's possible to have more than one phone."

"True...." My head is moving away from shock and into some kind of overdrive. The world isn't in slow motion anymore, it's in fast-forward times two. It's trying to tie every piece of evidence to him. "Does he drive a white car?" I ask.

"I've... never looked."

I sigh and finally chance looking away from Em to stare at my desk. I'm trying to remember all the things we've learned. At least if I'm focusing on that, I'm not focusing on the continuous questions raging inside my head. All those small details that Em always says are so important seem so hard to remember now. "The initial — *D* — it doesn't fit him. His name doesn't start with a D."

Em hands me the paper. "Be right back," she says, then heads to her room through the bathroom.

I take the couple of minutes she's gone to try to compose myself. I can't let all of this completely railroad me. I need to focus.

You can't find her if you completely spiral.

Em comes back with her laptop and takes her seat on the bed again. "His *last* name doesn't start with a D. What exactly do we know about him?"

"Not much. He's an English teacher."

"Exactly." She pulls up our school's website, then searches through the faculty roster. There he is: blonde hair, green eyes, a smile that's bright with eyes that now seem dull and lifeless. "Dorian."

My brain registers her saying his name, but it's distant and muffled, like someone talking in another room. I don't realize my fists are clenched until I attempt to relax my muscles. "What?" I say and pull my eyes from the screen again.

She highlights his name. "Dorian. That's his name." She looks at me. "That's gotta be where *D* comes from."

I stare at that highlighted line. It mocks me just as much as those crows do. The answer has been right here this whole time. A new thought occurs to me; if he really is *D,* then he has Abi. That means he's spent nearly a month watching his students be upset, consoling them, telling them things would work out, teaching us like nothing is wrong. Like he isn't harboring the very person everyone is mourning.

"We need to find out where he lives. We need to find Abi, find out where he's keeping her. We need to bring her home — make sure she's safe. We need to—"

Em interrupts the stream of consciousness spewing from me by shoving her hand over my mouth. "Stop." The grip her hand has is forceful, and it's enough to pull me back so I can take a much-needed deep breath.

She's right. Don't go down this road. You're back to finding answers, so it's time to buckle up and get those emotions in check again. You need a clear head.

"I'm sorry I didn't listen to you." She sounds so remorseful. It reminds me of Maddi at the café.

"Why? It's not your fault. You didn't do this, and you made good points when we were discussing things."

"So did you."

"But I didn't have solid evidence. I was speculating."

"You trusted your gut, though, and I should've listened," she says.

It doesn't matter now. We need to find Abi.

I grab my phone.

"What are you doing?" Em tries to peer over my shoulder at the screen, but I pull it away out of instinct.

"Texting Maddi."

"Why?"

I look up from my phone and lock eyes with her. "She deserves to know." Whether Maddi hates me or not, whether she said to leave her out of it or not, is irrelevant. This is her sister.

ME: NEED YOU HERE. ASAP.

MADELEINE: BUSY.

ME: PLEASE. IT'S IMPORTANT. IT'S ABOUT THE EVIDENCE.

MADELEINE: IT'S GONE.

MADELEINE: JUST LEAVE ME ALONE.

ME: PLEASE, I NEED YOU TO LISTEN.

MADELEINE: STOP TEXTING ME, HUNTER.

ME: MADDI, PLEASE. WE THINK WE KNOW WHO DID IT.

MADELEINE: ...

MADELEINE: TEN MINUTES.

TWENTY-SEVEN

Days since Abi's disappearance: 24

She said ten minutes but made it to the house in eight. Em barely had time to turn the knob when Maddi storms through. She's either on a mission or a war path, but I can't tell which.

"I thought all the evidence was gone. You just *suddenly* have a lead?"

Em looks at me with the warning of an incoming attitude, then back to Maddi. "Excuse you, *missy*, calm down. I don't know who put razor blades in your candy this year, but that's not how we're playing it in this house." She crosses her arms over her chest in a mirror of my stance. "Second, we found something that he didn't take but we weren't aware we had until now, *obviously*." That heavy silence settles between us. It's filled with such thick annoyance and tension that it's almost hard to breathe. When she's sure Maddi won't snap back with her own comment, Em nods toward the stairs. "C'mon."

The three of us go back up to my room, and Maddi and I take our usual spots on the bed, but this time Em sits between us with her laptop.

"Sorry about downstairs. I'm on edge," Maddi says.

"We all are." I can tell Em is trying to give her a reassuring smile, but it comes off insincere. "Here, look at this." Em hands Maddi the piece of stationery.

"So? It doesn't mean anything, remember?"

"That's what Hunter said. We don't know what the writing means, sure, but that stationery is from Mr. Clarke, and I'd put money on him being the one who left notes in her locker, and the one that was texting her."

Maddi scoffs. "How do you figure that?"

"Last week, Mr. Clarke had me take a note up to the office, and it was written on that stationery."

Maddi sighs while she processes what she's hearing. It's slow and calculated. She sounds so exhausted. "Realistically, anyone could have this stationery."

It's Em's turn to scoff. "Let's break this down then. How many people are going to have crow stationery? They're a great bird, don't get me wrong — love a good *murder* any day — but you have to admit it's not very likely that a lot of people have it. Add in the fact that whoever owns that *also* has to go to our school — or at least be on the grounds — *and* needs to be in Abi's life as more than just a random acquaintance and...." She holds out her hands toward the computer screen still housing Mr. Clarke's picture in a *ta-da* gesture.

I watch as the realization settles on Maddi's features. I can tell she's feeling as confused and angry and betrayed as I was earlier. How many times has Abi told us how wonderful he is? How many times were we subjected to rants and raves about the knowledge he's been giving her and how we're lucky to have him as a teacher?

He fooled all of us.

"I think I figured it out," I say despite Maddi's mouth opening to say something.

"Figured what out?" Em asks.

"The note! Din U-and-M eight. It's code—"

"Obviously," Em interrupts.

I give her a side glance then continue. "It's code, but it's probably a version of shorthand too. Din, diner or dinner. U-and-M, say it quickly. U-and-M, U&... me. 8, eight o'clock. Dinner, you and me, eight o'clock, or diner, you and me, eight o'clock."

They're both staring at me like I've grown a second head.

"What?" I ask.

"I just... don't see how you got there," Em says finally.

"The text messages talk about how he thought she was leaving notes specifically for him, and for reasons outside of school purposes. The journal mentioned how canceling plans on him caused problems, and he was getting aggressive. If she was leaving notes, it's not a far jump to assume he was leaving them back. If he did, this could've been one where he tried to make plans and she canceled."

"We need to go to the cops." Maddi says, as if Em and I aren't having a full conversation right next to her. There is no question in her words this time, and before either of us can say anything, she's standing and turning to face us again.

"I'm not going to the cops. Besides, we still need *solid* proof," I say.

"Isn't that what all this is?"

"No," Em says. "We have a suspect, reasonable suspicion, and circumstantial evidence. That isn't going to get the cops anywhere, not when they've decided she's just a runaway. They'll want hard evidence, especially if this is all we're giving them to go off of."

"There has to be *no question* that it's him." I say.

"So, what are we supposed to do?"

Em and I look at each other, then back to Maddi, to say in unison, "Get solid evidence."

"From a legal standpoint, all this piece of paper really proves is that Mr. Clarke *might* have left a note in Abi's locker. There's nothing tying him to the kidnapping, the texts, or anything else directly." I draw in a deep breath, stare at the highlighted name on the computer screen momentarily, then turn back to Maddi. "We need something that takes away all doubt."

"Like what?" Maddi crosses her arms. I can tell she's getting impatient. I'm not sure if it's a desire for all of this to be over or because it's not going her way, but she's not hiding the fact that she's unhappy with how things are happening.

Em and I don't say anything for a couple minutes. I don't know about her, but I'm running through every piece of evidence and every clue I can remember all over again. When something comes to mind, I snap my fingers. "Remember that squeal sound that Mr. Jenkins told me about? The one from the passenger side window? If Mr. Clarke's car does that, we can at least tie him to picking her up. That also allows for a tie to McMullins."

"Don't forget about the license plate." Em says.

"There's no proof that the white car from the photos is the same car from the night she was picked up," I say.

"You're right, but it certainly doesn't hurt if they have that R in the same place."

"Even if the license plate leads nowhere, we have a reason to suspect Mr. Clarke, which is reason enough to look into it, right?" Maybe I'm grasping at straws, maybe I'm making a mountain out of a molehill, but it could lead to bringing Abi home.

After losing all of that evidence, you owe it to her to see this through.

"Isn't that trick-or-treat thing at the school still going on tomorrow?" I ask.

"Yeah—oh." Em snaps her fingers. "Faculty are usually there."

"Yup, we can help with the cleanup. Maybe he'll need things taken to his car. If he does, we test the window. Then, all we need to do is follow him home to see if there's some kind of sign that he's keeping Abi there or where she might be," I say.

This could all work. All we need is to make him roll down his window. If we can confirm that, we got him — or at least have proof that he picked Abi up the night she disappeared.

"Alright, fine." Maddi glances between Em and me again, then settles on me. "We go to school, try to get evidence on Mr. Clarke, but we're *safe* and *smart* about it. If something fishy starts happening or anything like that, we—"

"Call the cops," Em and I cut her off to say in unison.

"We know," Em says while rolling her eyes. "We'll play it your way for now if that makes you happy. What's important is figuring out if he's really part of this."

Maddi seems satisfied with that answer, so I decide it's best not to tell her I disagree. With our last two rocky interactions, I'm really not in the mood for a third.

"We should make this look believable though. Maddi, we need to get you a costume," I say.

"Oh, she can borrow something from me!" Em's squeals in excitement and clutches her hands to her chest. To Em, dressing people up is better than playing with dolls.

"Like I was saying, get a costume for tomorrow. Em, call Cai and have him meet us there. We'll walk around together, make it look like we're there for the event."

"And the car window?" Maddi asks.

"Just be ready tomorrow night. I have a plan."

"Okay, can I bring Casey? Do you think that'll complicate things?"

Em and I both stop, look at each other, then back to Maddi. There's a slow growing smile that forms on my lips. "Is there a development? C'mon, spill."

Maddi hugs her middle and shrugs. "I-I guess so. We've been hanging out, and she's really fun. I know you said she's really hyper or whatever, but she's got this quiet and serious side too. Big heart, helpful, kind."

"Oh wait! Is this that waitress?" Em takes Maddi's arm and shakes it as a squeal erupts. The frequency is so high, part of me is convinced she's speaking whale. Sometimes I hate when Em gets excited. I never know if I'm going to get aquatic animal Em, or girlish, giggly Em, or tomboy Em — that one usually results in me getting punched. "OhmygodImsohappyforyou!"

"That's really great. Seriously," I say.

Maddi and I share a smile.

"Thanks. I like her. She... makes me happy. She's been really comforting during all of this." Her smile turns bashful as a blush creeps up her neck and invades her cheeks.

"Hey... I just want to say I'm sorry." My lips pull into a thin line as I try to figure out how to word my next few sentences. "For what happened at the school and here. I... I was taking things out on you, and you didn't deserve that."

"I get it. I mean, it wasn't okay, and you were a dick about things, but we're all dealing with a lot." She moves over to me and squeezes my shoulder. "I said things I shouldn't have too. You were stupid for not listening, but you're not to blame for someone breaking in and stealing things. This isn't your fault." The smile she offers me is warm and understanding and genuine. "We're good, Greene, just don't do it again."

A relieved, breathy laugh is my only response for a moment. "Deal."

TWENTY-EIGHT

Days since Abi's disappearance: 25

The night ends up going better than expected, the event was actually enjoyable. The kid's costumes are fun, a few of them try jumping out and scaring us. We scare some of them back, of course. There is bobbing for apples and trick-or-treating complete with the PTA moms handing out candy from the backs of their cars. Cai and Em dress up as Morticia and Gomez—

Called it.

—with Maddi and Casey opposing each other as a cat and mouse. I don't have anything prepared as a costume, so I end up slapping on some of Em's fake blood in random spots, then let it drip down my chin and throat to tell people I'm a new-age, not-so-incognito vampire.

As the night starts to wind down, I know it will be time to stick close to Mr. Clarke soon.

"The plan is simple," I remind them. "Offer to help carry things from the event out to his car. Em sneaks off to check the stationery against what we have from the journal, and after he's in the car but before he takes off, someone knocks on his passenger window to get him to roll it down."

"Sounds easy enough," Cai says. Until now, he and Casey didn't know what we'd been planning, but it doesn't take long to get them on board with the whole scheme. One thing I've always loved about Cai is his willingness to jump into our plans — especially if they're fun, interesting, or borderline illegal. Yet another reason Em and he make such a lovely pair. Reading Casey is still a bit of a conundrum, but after getting a reassuring nod from Maddi, she agrees.

"So, we're all in?" I look between the four of them but linger on Maddi. I can tell she's still not sure this will work, and it's clear she's wanting to bring up going to the cops again. Thankfully, she decides to keep it to herself. "If the window makes a noise, I'm following him back to the house."

Maddi opens her mouth, but I hold up a hand before she can get anything out.

"You do whatever you want, but I'm going to the house. End of story. I'm not giving this guy any more time to hurt Abi than he's already had."

There's defiance and resentment in her stare. Eventually, she lets out a huff and crosses her arms. "Alright, let's go," she says.

⁂

After packing everything up, Mr. Clarke only has a few boxes. They hold anything from leftover candy to a few stacks of cups and bowls to random decorations. We each grab a box and head out toward the parking lot, but about halfway down the hall, Em lets out a tut.

"Oh shoot!" Em says, loud and exaggerated. Luckily, Mr. Clarke doesn't know Em well enough to know her theatrical tones.

She's going for an Oscar this time.

"Is everything alright?" he asks.

"Yeah, I just forgot my phone in the classroom. I set it down when we were packing things up. You guys go ahead, I'll catch up. There can't be too many cars in the parking lot still, right?" She beams an overeager smile. "I'll find you."

Mr. Clarke looks hesitant at first, but when she doesn't break eye contact with him, he nods and turns to continue walking. Does he know we're on to the potential of him being involved with Abi's disappearance? Why does he seem so worried about someone being in the classroom without him?

"It was nice of you to stick around and help clean up. Thank you. Most students leave when the event ends," Mr. Clarke says as he lifts the trunk door. It's raised before I'm able to see the license plate, but, hey, we know he drives a white car now. He takes my box and sets it in the trunk.

"Not a problem." Cai says while flashing him a smile. His box is set next to mine before Mr. Clarke closes the trunk again. "Helping out makes things easier on you, right?"

"It does. How's the book report coming along for class, Mr. Greene?"

That was a weird switch.

"Almost done," I say.

Em is trotting toward us with her box. "Sorry it took so long." The small huff that leaves her sounds out of breath. It's not. I know Em's exercise sounds from years of racing down the sidewalk. This is worry. Something is off, or wrong. Did she manage to confirm something back in the classroom?

Mr. Clarke bounces his sights between the five of us after putting the last of the boxes in the backseat. He looks like a hunter scanning a pack of animals to find the weakest link. Is he testing us? Does he know we know something? His gaze lingers on Casey, and I swear I see his brows scrunch. That's when it dawns on me: they would've seen each other at the diner. Why hadn't any of us thought about bringing Casey around sooner? Why didn't any of us think about having her linger around school with us one day to see if she recognized anyone from that night?

My jaw clenches as I watch Mr. Clarke study Casey. He recognizes her, but his silence proves he can't place where.

You don't know who she is. Move on. Find someone else.

As if reading my thoughts, his eyes turn to Maddi before shifting to face her. Relief sweeps through me, but I see her back straighten. Out of one fire and into another. If Maddi can't calm herself down, she's going to give us all away. "You're Abigail's sister."

She nods and takes a small step toward Casey. Once Maddi is close enough, Casey reaches for her hand to lace their fingers. It makes me smile, seeing them together. The tension in Maddi's shoulders melts away the moment Casey's hand wraps around hers. It gives Maddi the reassurance she needs to keep going, but it doesn't take away the nervousness behind her eyes.

The longer I look at the two, the more I realize the change in Casey. Earlier in the night, she was laughing and having fun. Now, she looks on guard, like she's waiting for something to happen.

"She was in my class. I want to say I'm so sorry about what happened. I hope you're doing okay." His tone is more serious now, quieter. He's good at making himself sound concerned yet comforting.

That's how you pulled Abi in. You made her feel safe. You talked to her about your favorite books, asked her about hers. Made her think that you had innocent, pure intentions.

"Thank you." She tries to smile, but it's uneven. Given the circumstances, I hope he won't read too far into it.

"And your father? How's he getting along?" Mr. Clarke asks.

"Uh—he's... working a lot."

There's a moment of silence again where Mr. Clarke studies Maddi. On the outside, he looks like he's trying to gauge whether she needs more comfort or if he should say something else to offer her a sliver of peace, but behind his eyes is a calculating predator. He's testing her, trying to see if she knows anything or will crack under his pressure.

Don't do it, Maddi. Hold strong, you've got this. He won't hurt you with all of us here.

When she doesn't give in, Mr. Clarke draws in a deep breath and nods once. "Right, well, I should be getting home. Don't get into too much trouble." He waves, we wave back, and watch him get in his car.

Em takes this moment to study the car and nearly rams her elbow into my ribs. "Hunter, *look*."

I let out a small groan, press my hand against my side, and have half a mind to hit her back, but follow her gaze toward the car instead. More specifically, the car's license plate.

AR8 692

We glance at each other, then back to the car. It's not definitive, but it doesn't stop the rising adrenaline. I'd let myself get distracted earlier when he closed the trunk with the conversation he'd started.

The moment the engine is turned on, Em's jogging over to the passenger side and knocking on the window. When it doesn't roll down right away, she turns to look at us over her shoulder, then turns back. She seems concerned. Bending at the waist, she knocks on the window again and this time, he rolls it down almost immediately. A high-pitched squeal comes from somewhere inside the door.

I'm trying to listen to what Em is saying, but they're too far away, and any chance of catching the conversation is interrupted by Maddi pulling my sleeve.

"Did you hear it?" She takes a step closer to me.

Of course, I did.

Before I can say anything, Casey is standing behind us both. "That's him. I-I didn't want to say anything or give it away when he was over here, but that's him. *That's* the guy that Abi came into the diner with."

My stomach has a mini gymnast taking up residence and training for the biggest competition of their life. It was Mr. Clarke that picked her up that night. He's the *him* from the texts. He's the *him* she was meeting. The *him* from the notes.

Mr. Clarke. He's D. For sure.

We all smile and wave to Mr. Clarke as he backs out of the parking spot and takes off.

"Please don't do this," Maddi pleads. "Don't go over there. We know now. We can go to the cops and tell them we have a lead. We can tell them who we think did this."

Em gives me an expression that clearly reads *give me the keys so I can get the car* as she walks back over to us. The keys are tossed to her before I turn back to Maddi. "I'm going. I want *physical* proof that he's connected. No more maybes. I want to be sure that if and when we go to the cops, he's being put away for good. If you don't want to come, that's fine. I'm sure Cai can take you home. Em and I will follow him and keep you updated."

I'm relieved, and a little surprised, when she agrees to go with Cai. Part of me assumes it's because Casey is there, and she either doesn't want to get her involved too much or doesn't want Casey to see her get into it with me. Either way, when she agrees, I give them a quick wave and take off at a sprint toward the car.

Twenty-Nine

— • —

Days since Abi's disappearance: 25

My door isn't even closed when the tires squeal under the pressure of the gas.

"Did you see which way he went?"

"Make a right out of the parking lot," I say.

Em doesn't slow down to make the turn, causing me to slam into the middle console. "Jesus, Em, we're not going to be able to do anything if we die on the way there."

"He's already a good two or three blocks ahead of us, Hunter. We need to figure out which way he went." We're going double the speed limit when she has to slam on the breaks at a red light. The only things that stops me from hitting the dashboard are quick reflexes and locking my elbows. "This road only goes straight—"

"For another half a mile."

She glares at me. "That's what I'm saying."

I wait to see if she's going to interrupt me again. When she doesn't, I continue. "It goes straight for another *half a mile,* then banks off to the right. We'll catch him." Annoyance is seeping into my tone before I can stop it.

Once the light turns green, she hits the gas so hard the tires squeal. The curve of the road isn't sharp enough for us to flip if she doesn't slow down, but it's definitely enough for me to need the handle above the door. As soon as the curve settles, we see him.

"Don't get too close," I warn and sink into my seat a little as if that's going to stop him from seeing the car.

"I know what I'm doing." Her hands grip the steering wheel a little tighter and the leather squeaks.

Is she readying herself for a chase? There isn't a reason for Mr. Clarke to suspect anyone's following him, and he doesn't know what car we drive... does he? I think back to the pictures on Abi's phone and the white car in the background. I'm usually the one that drives us around, and I pick her up for dates. If he's been following us for that long, he knows.

"Em, stay farther back." My voice is at a lower volume this time. "If he's been following Abi and me...." My words trail off as Mr. Clarke's car slows down. She immediately understands without me having to finish my sentence.

Thank whoever needs to be thanked for twin telepathy.

"I didn't think about that part. We should've driven Cai's car," I say.

"Can't fix it now."

When Mr. Clarke makes a right, Em takes us down one more street before turning.

"What are you doing?"

"This neighborhood is set up like a grid. If he goes down the road and we don't see him at the next cross-street, he stayed in that section. If he makes a turn, we make a turn." She has this down. I never would've thought of that.

Where did you learn all of this? Detective shows don't teach this kind of stuff. Are you moonlighting without me?

When we come to the stop sign, I look to the right and Mr. Clarke is pulling through the intersection.

"See?"

"Maddi was right. You are a little scary sometimes," I say.

"Don't get all sentimental on me now, Hunter." She glances my way with a mischievous smirk, then back to the road. At the next stop sign, there's no Mr. Clarke. With a couple turns, we circle back to the row of houses we lost him in.

"There! On the left." I point across her line of sight causing her to slap my hand away.

"Do you want us to crash!?" She drives us a couple houses down, circles back around again, and parks. "Well... what's the plan from here?"

I don't immediately answer and instead lean forward for a better view of the house. Mr. Clarke's getting out of the car and heading inside the house without any boxes or leftover supplies from the school.

I don't have a plan for this. Not yet.

"You think we could get him back out of the house?" I ask. "Call him and pretend that he's needed back at the school or there's an emergency somewhere?" It works in movies and on TV, doesn't it? Em's words run through my head — "this is real life." She's right, it is. We don't get to walk out of a theater when all of this is over and know that life is going back to the way it was. As much as I want there to be, there's no more "going back to normal." Normal removed itself as an option a long time ago.

"Maybe, but do *you* have his number? Because I don't," Em quips.

Dang it.

The only number I have is for *D,* and that's the last thing I want to dial. Not to mention, it was out of service the last time we tried calling it. I sit in silence, staring at the house, and willing Mr. Clarke to leave again.

Hang on, Abi, I'm going to get you out of there.

"I... we should come back tomorrow," she says.

"No." I finally look at Em. "I'm not waiting anymore. It's been weeks. What if she's hurt? What if he's doing something to her? What if she's—" I stop and open the door. The thought of her being dead is enough to make me want to sprint to the house.

"Wait—"

"Em, listen, we've waited long enough. *Abi* has waited long enough. If I need to knock on the door and confront him head on, I will, but this ends. *Tonight.*"

Right before I step out of the car, a dog starts barking. My eyes dart back to the house to see the door opening and a black Labrador bounding out of the house with Mr. Clarke in tow. I immediately swing the door back — stopping it before it can slam — and sink down in the seat. When I notice Em still in full view, I pull her down by the shoulder of her shirt.

"Hey!" My hand covers her mouth to muffle the ending of her yell.

"SHH—*shut up.*"

After a moment, I peek over the dashboard to see the dog and Mr. Clarke walking the opposite way down the sidewalk. "Stay here, keep watch. I'm going inside. When you see him coming back, call me."

Em draws in a breath to say something.

"No, Emerald. I'm serious. Stay here, keep wa—" She cuts me off.

"Hunter Mateo." She waits until she has my full attention. "I was going to say 'take this'." She hands me her not-a-pen knife. "Just in case. The stationery matched. It's him... just be careful."

I smile. "You're always so good to me."

"Ew, get out of the car." She shoves me toward the door.

THIRTY

Days since Abi's disappearance: 25

The door's unlocked.

Is it breaking and entering if it's unsecured?

Probably. It's still private property.

Once inside, I try to map out a plan for all of this. From what I can see, it has the remnants of the cookie-cutter set up every other house has. I pull out my phone, turn on the flashlight, and keep it pointed toward the ground. I don't need the neighbors seeing a random light on and alerting Mr. Clarke or the cops.

"Think," I say to myself, then turn and look around the living room. The colors are bland, and the room is set up for functionality rather than comfort. Either he doesn't spend much time here or he chooses not to invest in making his home inviting.

I have to figure out what I'm supposed to be searching for. I don't expect him to keep her tied up in the dining room or to find a giant neon sign blinking *she's over here, come get her*. That would be too easy, but there has to be something that gives away if she's here and where.

Try to find anything that ties him to her first. Something to prove he's D. The phone, another piece of the stationery. Something.

At a quick glance, the hallway appears normal. Pictures line the walls and scatter across a long, thin table set up against one of the walls. However, the longer I study them, the more I see that they're not personalized photos, they're the stock photos that come in most frames. There are different families or couples, all in different stages of laughter or enjoyment. It's not until I look at a larger frame with a collage of photos that I see one picture that could be Mr. Clarke's. There's a younger version of him standing in between a man and woman. The woman has the same round face and that same blonde hair and green eyes. The male is tall, thin, and has dark hair with even darker eyes. Is that his father?

He looks menacing.

A noise from somewhere outside jolts me from my thoughts.

Keep moving. You're not here to snoop, and he could be back any minute.

I need to work faster, smarter. He won't keep incriminating evidence out in the open.

He'd want it hidden somewhere but in a place with easy access.

A bedroom? An office? I make my way up the stairs and look around.

There are two bedrooms upstairs: the master bedroom at the top of the stairs and a standalone at the end of the hall. Being caught in one of these rooms means getting cornered. The thought makes my throat tighten. I don't want to be stuck in a bedroom when Mr. Clarke comes home. What if I have to freefall from the second-story window, get hurt, and can't make it out of the yard without being seen?

I go into the room at the end of the hall to find an office. It smells like old books and mothballs, and it reminds me of a nursing home. My nose wrinkles. "Gross."

The back wall is lined with several packed bookshelves, but off to the right is a desk covered in ungraded papers with three drawers down the right side. I decide the desk is probably the best place to start. The first couple drawers are normal — notebooks, pens, loose leaf paper, folders — but when I try to open the bottom drawer, it doesn't budge.

Why would you keep this one locked?

Logic says it's probably tax paperwork or something of that nature, but I'm not leaving here without knowing I've found everything I can. I pull out Em's knife and pry the door open. It's going to tip him off to someone being in the house, but if it means finding Abi... My thoughts trail off when I see the contents of the drawer.

I prop my phone on the desk chair with the flashlight facing me and pull out a few papers to reveal a couple of handwritten notes and a pink scrunchy at the bottom of the drawer. I read a couple of the notes and find they're all from Abi. I've spent almost four years reading her writing, I know it anywhere. The papers are set on the floor next to me. When I look in the drawer again, I spot a small black phone, and pick it up to examine it.

Who carries around a phone like this anymore? It's old school; no touch screen, no internet, probably barely capable of sending a text. Usually, they're a burner phone according to Em. I turn it on, watch the screen come to life, and open the text messages. There's only one thread saved.

"Abi."

It's her number, but I need to *be sure* that this is the number she saved for *D*. It doesn't take long to scroll through the messages before I start seeing familiar words. The manipulation and fake apologies, the lines he fed her to twist the situation into something in his favor. It's all there.

We got him.

I shove the phone in my pocket before putting the rest of the drawer's contents back, closing it, and grabbing my phone.

ME: IT'S HIM.

ME: FOUND THE CELL, HE HAS SOME OF ABI'S SCHOOL PAPERS.

EMERALD: ARE YOU SURE IT'S THE PHONE? AND HE'S A TEACHER, OF COURSE HE'S GOING TO HAVE SOME OF HER SCHOOL PAPERS.

ME: YOU THINK A TEACHER WOULD KEEP PAPERS FROM ONLY ONE STUDENT LOCKED IN A DRAWER WITH AN ANCIENT FLIP PHONE THAT ONLY HAS CORRESPONDENCE WITH THAT ONE PERSON? WITH THAT PERSON'S CONTACT SAVED AS "A. PERKINS"?

ME: I CHECKED THE TEXTS TO MAKE SURE. IT'S THE SAME PHONE.

EMERALD: BE CAREFUL.

ME: I'M GOING TO FIND HER. SHE HAS TO BE HERE.

ME: KEEP WATCH.

I search the closet in the office, then move back down the hall to the master bedroom. He isn't stupid enough to keep her in a bedroom, I'm sure of it, but I check under the bed and in the closets anyway. Even if she's not there, there's a chance I'll stumble on the stuff that was taken from my house.

You need to move faster. She's got to be here somewhere, and he's going to be back any minute.

I jog back downstairs and look down one side of the hallway, then the other. There isn't anything in the living room, probably nothing in the dining room.

Where does this go?

On the left-hand side of the hallway is a door — a door that other houses don't usually have. When it opens, I'm greeted with stairs.

"A basement." I glance over my shoulder toward the front door. Going down there means it'll be harder to get out of the house if Mr. Clarke comes back before I can leave.

Not any harder than being upstairs and having to jump out the window. Abi could be down there.

I've come this far, I can't stop now. With the door closed behind me, I head down and am slapped with the smell of wet earth. It smells like freshly dug soil and makes the pit of my stomach turn sour.

So, he has an unfinished basement. An unfinished basement with exposed and possibly disrupted dirt. That could be an open or recently covered grave. I hate this.

I'm not a religious person, but I say a silent prayer that Abi is still alive and okay.

Pausing at the bottom of the stairs, I look around. The room I step into is roughly twenty-by-thirty feet and unfinished, literally. Most of the walls are still dirt, and where there isn't dirt, there's concrete that looks like it was laid out by an amateur. It's sturdy enough to hold its shape and not collapse the room above it, but it's very obviously a home project.

On the far left is an old, worn dresser with a dirty mattress on a metal bed frame next to it. It resembles something someone would collected from the trash that they haven't gotten around to washing yet. Is this where he's been keeping her? Is this the way she's been living for all this time? "There's not even a pillow or sheet on the bed."

A muffled noise catches my attention off to the right.

"Abi!" I dart toward her.

THIRTY-ONE

Days since Abi's disappearance: 25

"Oh my god," I say.

She's tied to a chair with a table nearby housing a TV playing a sitcom. I drop to my knees in front of her, set my phone against the TV so the flashlight shines on her, and turn back. My hands cup her cheeks. I look her over and try to find evidence of anything that would stop her from being able to escape. She has bruises on her arms and legs, but no cuts. That's a good sign. She doesn't have broken bones or gashes or other major injuries.

Her hair's been changed from brown to a dark auburn, and she's wearing a dirty sundress with strapped sandals. Has she been in these the whole time? These aren't her clothes. I've never seen her in a dress before. Abi always calls them impractical because they don't offer a lot of protection from the elements. I can see tears forming in her eyes as something between a laugh and a sob comes. She's shaking her head, her eyes are so wide I can see the whites all around her iris'. She's trying to say something, but a wad of cloth shoved in her mouth muffles her words. I try to imagine what she's feeling: terror, relief? A mixture of both?

"Sh—sh, I'm going to get you out of here." The gag in her mouth is the first thing to go. "Are you hurt?"

She ignores my question and says, "Oh my god, Hunter, you need to leave. You can't be here. He'll hurt you, please." She's panicking. Her eyes lift to search the ceiling as if she can see through the floor above us then back to me. Her breathing is frantic, and if she doesn't calm down, she's going to send herself into a panic attack or pass out.

"He'll kill you, *please.*" The tears in her eyes tell me they're from distress over something happening to me, not the happiness and relief of being rescued. There's a new ache in my chest now, but this time it carries a heaviness I can't place.

"I'm not leaving you." I say and pat my pockets then hoodie searching for the knife Em gave me. It isn't here.

Shoot. I probably left it in the office... great.

"You have to listen to m—"

I cut her off and say, "Abi, stop. I'm taking you home."

She seems so different: sunken in eyes that are lined with dark circles and hold a fear she never had before. The sparkle that came with the way she looked at the world is gone. She's a shell of the girl I knew, and I hate Mr. Clarke for doing this to her.

One of my hands lifts but before it can reach its destination, she flinches away. I watch as horror flashes through her, then realization that I'm not who her mind tries to tell her I am.

"I'm sorry." She sounds so small, so broken, and I can still hear the panic underneath.

"Don't apologize." I say then start working on the knotted rope around one of her wrists. I have so many questions, but there isn't time to ask them.

"Is he home? How did you get in here?"

"He's walking his dog, he left the door unlocked," I say and tap her wrist to signal it's free. "Work on the other one. I'll get your ankles."

"You really need to leave," she says, but she's untying her other wrist, anyway.

"Why did he even do this?" I ask, ignoring her plea. I'm not leaving her, so there's no point in arguing.

With a defeated sigh, she says, "I-I guess he's... in love with me? He's talked about how he knows I'm in love with him, not you, how you're keeping me hostage in our relationship and I'm afraid to tell you the truth. That our love is forbidden, but he's going to take me away from here so we can be together. That my notes are what tipped him off — that I left him codes in the notes — that he's going to give me the life I deserve." The more she rambles off the reasons, the louder the ringing in my ears becomes. More anger is hitting me. Anger and frustration and resentment.

How dare he!

"How did you find me?"

I glance up before starting the last restraint. I want to tell her everything that's happened, everything that we've gone through to get to this point, but there isn't time yet. It's the knowledge that we'll be able to sit and be safe and talk and hold each other is the only thing keeping me going. "Good ol' fashion detective work."

She lets out a scoff that's meant to be a laugh and pulls her wrist free.

"I had a lot of help. Maddi and Em. I couldn't have done it without them."

"Remind me to send a thank-you card to Em." With both her legs untied, we stand, and I grab my phone with one hand while my other takes her to lace our fingers.

"She's in the car, you can tell her in person." I wish there's a pause button to push on everything around us. I wish there could be *one* moment where we can reunite and nothing is threatening to end the moment prematurely.

There will be plenty of time for that later. This is the hard part, getting out of the house. Right now, you need to get her home.

Anxiety floods me again. What if we're caught trying escape? Is Mr. Clarke's dog trained to attack? Is it a friendly "family" dog? That tightness in my chest comes back, but before my own panic can set in, it's shoved to the back of my mind.

You can break down and freak out later. There are more important things to focus on.

"C'mon."

We are halfway up the stairs when my phone starts vibrating. "Shi—" The sudden sensation startles me. The moment it hits the ground, everything goes black. I'm halfway to picking up the phone when it hits me; that had to have been Em. She's probably calling to say she sees Mr. Clarke.

"Seriously, Hunter?" Abi says.

I let go of her hand and attempt to turn the phone on. Nothing. Abi lets out a small, sarcastic laugh.

This can't be happening.

"That did *not* just happen." Even through the darkness, she finds and shoves me. "Are we in a badly written horror movie? The boy finally rescues the girl, but as they escape their only communication with the outside world is destroyed because the boy gets startled and drops the cellphone." Abi's quickly written narration makes me roll my eyes.

I don't say anything right away and use the moments of silence to put my phone back in my pocket. "I want to say this is all a bad joke, but..." I shake my head despite her not being able to see me. "We need to go. *Now.*" I grab Abi's hand again and nearly drag her up the stairs the rest of the way.

With the door thrown open, we dart down the hallway. It doesn't look like anyone is home yet. Hopefully they're still a minute or two away and we can sneak out the backdoor.

We're halfway down the hallway when *her* voice surfaces. I pull us both to a halt. It's muffled and I can't make out full sentences, but I'd know it anywhere.

Em. She must be trying to buy us time.

"It sounds... but I... help." I wish I could make out what Em's saying.

Mr. Clarke replies, but before Em can speak again, there's the distinct thud of something hitting wood. Did they start to fight? Did something happen to Em? A new wave of adrenaline is coursing through me so quickly I'm vibrating, and the thoughts swirling around my head are playing a game of tug-o-war. Half of me is screaming to go help Em, to make sure she's okay, while the other half reminds me that Abi still needs my help.

I only snap out of my thoughts when the door handle starts to turn.

Crap—no!

"Go—go—*go*," I say and shove Abi toward the steps leading upstairs. It's the opposite direction we need to go, but the dining room is still ten feet down the hallway, and we'll never make it without being seen.

THIRTY-TWO

Days since Abi's disappearance: 25

"C'mon, Max, let's get you some dinner," Mr. Clarke says as we reach the top of the stairs. There's a bark in response to his words. Mr. Clarke sounds a little out of breath, but that could be because of the walk, right? Not some altercation outside?

Abi pulls me into the office, and we head straight for one of the closets.

My mind races with thoughts of Em again. Where is Em? What happened outside? Did Em walk away and go back to the car? I have to find her, but first, Abi and I need to get out of this house.

What're we supposed to do now?

"Hunter... the door. We left the door to the basement open." The worry in her words is enough to bring me back to the present, but it's the grip on my forearm that really gets my attention. Strong, constricting. She's silently begging me for help. She's terrified. The way she looks up at me reminds me of Maddi holding onto her cup in the café.

You should've followed what Maddi suggested — going to the cops. Look at you now; stuck in an upstairs closet, waiting for the guy who kidnapped your girlfriend to figure out she's missing and neither of you have a way out of the house.

I push the thoughts away. I need to be strong. For her. "Don't worry, it's going to be f—"

"Abigail!" The word brings a chill up my spine. He's found the door. The shout causes Max to bark a couple of times. "Abi, where are you?" Contrasting the first call of her name, this time he's talking normally.

Just like in the text messages. One moment he's angry, the next he's normal.

When I crack the door open, Abi pulls at my arm in a silent protest. "It's fine." I stick my head out of the door, look around the room then back to her. If I know where he is, we can avoid him. "We're going to sneak back downstairs. Once you're down there, I want you to run. Don't look back, don't worry about me. *Run.* Go outside, find Em, get to the car."

She takes a step toward me and presses her chest against my arm. I can feel how hard her heart is beating.

"No matter what, okay? Run." I step out of the closet.

Normally, I'd find heavy footsteps annoying. They make everything shake, it's disturbing to the people around you. However, this is one time where it's helpful, and, boy, does Mr. Clarke stomp his feet.

Top of the stairs, on the landing... coming down the hallway.

I push Abi back toward the closet, and just as I close the door, Mr. Clarke enters the room. Her nails dig into my forearm, lighting my nerves on fire, and the shudder of her breathing taps against the side of my arm. There's silence for a moment, then the sound of an office door slamming against the wall a few times from his anger. It makes us both jump, but we stay silent.

"Abi." The level of sudden calm his tone takes is even more terrifying than his yelling. In any other situation, I'd assume he's being genuine and honest. The words sound kind and warm and welcoming. He's mastered this part of things.

"I'm not going to hurt you, okay? I forgive you for trying to run away, it's because you're scared. It takes time to adjust to change, to a new life." There's shuffling around the room. "I thought you understood. I thought we talked everything out last time. You promised you wouldn't do this anymore..." his words trail off and are replaced with a sigh.

"Abi... please. It doesn't need to be this way. I don't want to keep having to tie you up downstairs. I want us to have dinners together and watch movies together — go back to the diner." I hear him open the closet on the opposite side of the room. "Come out, come out, wherever you are." His words come out in a sing-song way meant to be playful, but after a moment of silence, he slams the door closed in more anger. "Damn it, where are you?"

His feet pound against the floor as he crosses the room and pauses in front of the closet we're hiding in. I grab the doorknob in some feeble attempt to hope I can keep the door from opening. My heart hammers faster. Abi's nails dig into my skin further. My jaw clenches and my nostrils flare.

She's scared. Just stay quiet.

She's shaking violently and a glance her way shows a wide-eyed stare locked on the door. I don't know the extent of what Mr. Clarke has done to her, but whatever it is, it's enough to make her petrified of the man.

He could've done a million and one things to her in the last few weeks to make her like this. Starved her, beat her...

There's one thing I'm praying he hasn't done.

The sound of glass shattering echoes from across the house.

"Abi!" He releases the doorknob. His footsteps tell us he's dashing out of the room and down the hall. I stare at the floor, focusing on the sliver of light eking under the door, in disbelief that he decided against checking the closet, but I'm pulled back by Abi's words.

"We need to leave."

She's right. A breath I don't know I'd been holding leaves me in a rush before I push the door open slowly to try to prevent any creaking. I do a quick scan of the room to make sure it's clear then we're out and tip-toeing toward the hall again.

"Abi?"

I poke my head through the threshold of the door in time to see Mr. Clarke walking into the master bedroom. Sure, the bedroom is at the top of the stairs, but if we can get there quick enough, we might be able to get down the stairs and out the door before he can catch us.

"*Go.*" I say and push her forward. There's no hesitation. We're running down the hallway, Abi's sandals slap against the floor in loud claps, but stealth doesn't matter anymore. Mr. Clarke emerges from the bedroom and when it registers that she's not alone, there's a darkness that takes him over. His expression is wild, feral. I've never seen him look so angry. I've never seen *anyone* look so angry.

Run. Run! Don't look back. Just keep moving.

Abi makes it to the landing and is about to step onto the first stair when Mr. Clarke's hand grabs her upper arm and yanks her back. She stumbles into him and immediately pushes against his chest screaming, but he's stronger than her, and I'm not close enough to help yet.

"No! Stop!" There's a sob somewhere in her angered words.

"I don't want to do this, Abigail. I want us to be happy!"

I don't stop the momentum of my run. Instead, I barrel ahead and ram a shoulder against Mr. Clarke. It's enough to break the hold he has on Abi, but not enough to knock him down. "Go!"

Abi turns, letting her flight instinct take over, and then everything happens all at once:

Loud barking and the sound of nails on wood announces Max's arrival.

He skids around the corner, then takes off up the stairs without hesitation.

He lunges at her.

Abi screams.

"No!" My knee slams against Mr. Clarke's groin before I shove myself away and reach for Abi.

She's too far away.

Abi's desperate attempts to grab the banister fail causing her and Max to tumble down the stairs in a series of yelps and whimpers. She hits the floor at the bottom of the stairs.

THIRTY-THREE

Days since Abi's disappearance: 25

The sound that rings out when she lands hits me like a punch to the gut, and echoes around my head. For a few, brief moments, the world is silent. Everything stops.

I don't remember making it the rest of the way down the stairs, but the impact of the floor against my knees makes it obvious I dropped to them when I reach her. There's a whimper off to my right with a high-pitched whine that comes with staggered breathing. My eyes dart toward Max, but he doesn't seem like an immediate threat, so my attention goes back to Abi.

"Wake up." My hands cup her face, move to her shoulders, shake her. "Abi, *please.*" The longer she lays there motionless, the more my mind spirals into panic.

No, this isn't happening. She'll wake up. She's fine. She's only knocked out. Everything's okay. It'll all be okay.

Abi, darling, *Mi Vida.* We've overcome so much and look where we are. Look at what's happened. I found you, searched so hard for you....

Don't give up now. Please... please wake up.

Unexpected hands yank me backward and toss me to the ground.

"Get away from her!" Mr. Clarke is already leaning over her when I push myself into a seated position. He's pressing his face near hers and resting his forehead against her chest. I can't tell if she's breathing, but the frustrated yell he lets out says something is wrong. After a moment, Mr. Clarke turns his head and stares at me with narrowed eyes. Anger. No, fury. There's nothing but unbridled fury.

Get up. You need to get up. Get to a phone, call the police. Do SOMETHING. Don't sit there, you idiot!

But I can't make myself move. I'm paralyzed and staring at a motionless version of Abi with our deranged English teacher hovering over her.

Without warning, Mr. Clarke lunges at me.

"You did this!" He screams.

Watching him come toward me kicks my body into gear. I'm up and on my feet, but my scramble is frantic and messy. I skid across the floor while my hand automatically grabs the molding on the threshold of the living room to propel myself into the room.

"You just couldn't let her go! You had to come looking for her!" He's only feet behind me and closing the gap quickly.

I jump over the couch and turn to face him. "You can't take people. You can't keep and collect them. They're not objects!" I don't know when my own anger surfaces, but it's evident. Oh, boy, is it evident. My heart is racing again, my chest heaves.

That switch flips again and what used to be anger moves into rage. A new dose of adrenaline surges through me, and where the world was once dull and quiet from shock, it's now wild and brilliant and loud.

"You don't get it," he says amid a laugh, "oh, of course not. How could you? You think you *own* her, that she'll never want or be with anyone but you. I didn't take her, she *wanted* to come with me. She practically begged for it. She didn't want to be with you, Hunter. She wanted to be with *me*."

He moves around the couch, but for every step forward he takes, I step back. If I can keep him talking, if I can distract him for long enough, maybe I can back myself toward the front door and escape. I can leave and get to a neighbor's house or yell for help.

"Then why was she planning to go to college with me, huh? Why were we planning a life together?" I bump into a side table causing a lamp to crash to the floor but keep moving backward. The room is dimmer now. In any other circumstance, I'd be thankful for the shroud of darkness, but he knows this place better than I do. He has the advantage here.

"Think about it. Going to BCC means being close to me," he says. "It means we continue seeing each other. Those notes she left me? 'Meet me after school, I want to discuss this assignment' and 'I really need to talk to you about this grade.' They were little ways to see me. They were excuses she gave us both in case anyone asked why we were spending so much time together." He tries to close the gap with a few quick steps toward me, but I side-step away from him, running into the wall in the process.

This isn't going to work. I need to put more distance between us. I glance to the side and around the room, but when there's another shuffle of steps, I turn back and take off out of the room, down the hall. When I look back at him again, I can see the calculation behind his eyes. He's waiting until I'm paying the least amount of attention, and that's when he'll try attacking again. We're at a standstill — both in the hallway, refusing to take our eyes off each other in case the other tries something.

"Why do you think I found a diner out of town? No one knew us there, we could be ourselves," he says.

"But she still didn't want you, did she?" I can't help the scoff that comes through the words. "She *still* didn't want anything to do with you. You're her teacher, and, honestly, it's fucking creepy the way you pine after her." The last sentence recharges his anger, and he runs toward me again. Turning on my heels, I run further down the hallway. I need to think of a plan. I need to find a way to

—

The backdoor! If I can manage to get through the dining room, I can get out the backdoor.

I'm five feet from the dining room with Mr. Clarke seconds behind me when the distinct sound of four-legged running comes from my left. There's a singular shout from Mr. Clarke, a bark, and the next thing I know, I'm on the ground with a sharp pain in my left forearm. The pressure of Max's bite is vicious, but it's the whipping of his head that thrashes me back and forth, making stabilizing my arm impossible. The more he rips the skin, the more pain settles in.

"Get off me!" I yell and grab Max's snout. I read somewhere that pinning an animal's cheeks against their teeth causes enough pain for them to want to release whatever they're holding, but apparently Max doesn't fit that standard. The more I press, the harder he clamps. I try to stay calm. Despite my best efforts, a cry of pain leaves me.

"Max, release," Mr. Clarke finally says, and when Max does, my arm is dripping blood and multiple puncture wounds have left the skin and muscle shredded.

I turn and crawl across the floor—

I need to keep moving.

—but before I can attempt to make it back to my feet, Mr. Clarke kicks me forward, and I land facedown on the tile.

"You tried to take her from me," he says as his foot collides with my side. I let out a grunt that turns into a cough and turn onto my side to curl into a fetal position. I'm a fighter, but it's hard to fight when your lungs stop working.

I'm still gasping for breath when he uses his foot to push me onto my back. He's standing over me with a grin so demented he looks like a comic book villain. Wide, wild eyes with features that are terrifyingly gleeful.

"I'll make sure you can never do that again."

Get off your ass NOW, Greene!

I try to turn back onto my stomach so I can get away. Mr. Clarke straddles me before I get the chance. His hands find my throat and tighten. I gasp for air while my hands grab at his wrists.

They squeeze, claw, pull. It feels futile. He's stronger than I expect, stronger than me.

"Stop struggling. It'll just make this harder." His teeth are clenched, but that doesn't stop the spit that sprays when he talks. His grip cuts into my throat so much, my eyes widen. I swear they're going to pop out of their sockets, and the pressure hurts more than any headache I've ever experienced.

My lungs are burning, screaming, for air. Panic is starting to rise, but I turn my focus from his hands to his face. My fists swing wildly, but between my injured arm and the growing black spots now taking over the world around me, the most I accomplish is pushing him to grip harder. He lifts my head and shoulders only to slam me back against the tile. My head bounces. The impact causes a high-pitched ringing.

My mouth slacks open as my eyes roll back. I thought the dog bite hurt, that was nothing. Real pain comes from my brain pressing against my skull and fighting to get out. The building pressure in my head combines with this new impact making it feel like my head's going to explode. When I'm finally able to focus, I claw at his hands and wrists again.

"S-stop...." The word is weak. There's not a lot of breath left in my lungs, but I can't give up.

Don't you dare let him kill you.

"Why would I do that? Huh? Tell me, Hunter." He leans forward, and I can somehow smell his breath — hot and sour — as it covers my face. The edges of my vision are blurring, my lungs are starting to give up their fight for fresh air.

Do something!

I try to. I try to hit him again. The heels of his hands press down further, and the panic taking over intensifies. I can't force a breath between the grip on my throat and caving of my windpipe.

This is it. It's going to snap. I have come this far, done so much, only to be overpowered and killed by a pathetic, obsessive, insane man.

"What? Don't have a witty answer this time?" he shouts. His hands pick me up to slam me back down again. Another collision, another bounce of my head against tile, only this time I can hear a crack just before my hair becomes warm and wet. The world goes black. Everything hurts. Why am I so tired all of a sudden?

A nap wouldn't be so bad...

The burning in my lungs has subsided.

Am I able to breathe again? At least he let me go.

The pain in my head is ebbing away, and a light, cottony feeling replaces it.

Man, that was a horrible headache.

Some of my vision comes back, but the edges remain black and inky. "P-ple..." I can't finish the word, the rest of my air is gone, and my voice is failing me.

Someone laughs in the distance.

Something slams in another room.

Seconds later, there's yelling.

What is he saying now?

I can't focus on the words.

I attempt another gasp.

My arms try to move, but they're filled with lead.

My body reminds me that sleep is a wonderful idea.

No! Don't go to sleep! Stay awake!

I try to force my eyes open, but the harder I fight, the darker the world seems to get.

More yelling.

Another loud noise.

A weight drops on me....

Thirty-Four

— · —

Days since Abi's disappearance: 26

Waking up feels like my soul is being slapped back into my body. It's sudden and hard and it *hurts*. A deep breath fills my lungs, and for a moment I'm not sure where I am because of the blinding lights of the room.

"Good morning, sleepy head." Maddi says.

Are you yelling? Stop yelling.

"Hey." I wince at the effort to speak. My throat feels like sandpaper.

"Yeah, looks like I'll be getting a few days of silence for the first time since our shared months in the womb." Em's smirking when I look at her. She's sitting in a chair to my right a couple of feet away and has a bandage on the left side of her forehead accompanied by a couple scratches on her face. "Mom will be glad you're awake. She's been nothing but a pacing, babbling mess since the cops called her. She was furious at first, but once she learned what happened and why, she calmed down a little."

"Where is she?" I push myself up on the bed a little farther, and pain courses through my forearm. When I look down, there are heavy, white bandages wrapping the area. There's a vague memory of a dog thrashing and ripping, pain. When an attempt to remember anything else is made, it's hazy and confusing. With the pounding in my head growing, my right hand presses to the side of my head.

More bandages.

My hand shifts around but the moment it gets to the back of my head, sharp pain hits. Flashes of Mr. Clarke on top of me, choking me, slamming me back against the tile brings me back to the night before. I can feel the panic rising again, but a deep breath settles it. Not a lot, but enough.

You're at the hospital. You're fine.

"She's down the hall talking to Officer Samson. Oh, by the way, they were pissed you took the phone. I mean, *I* get why you took it — proof and all — but it's evidence that was tampered with. Not to mention they didn't find it until the paramedics turned over your clothes. Hope you weren't too attached to those."

I scoff. Judging by the way she says her last sentence, they probably cut them off. "Wh-what... happened?"

Stop talking. It hurts.

"To me or you?" It comes out sarcastic, but Em's asking a genuine question.

I shrug, not wanting to irritate my throat further. I watch the two share a glance before Maddi stands and grabs a cup of water from the tray near the bed to hand to me. The look between them is off somehow. I can't put my finger on it, but I can tell there's something they're holding back. What are they hiding? Why are they hiding it?

"After I tried calling the second time and your phone went straight to voicemail, I decided to create some kind of diversion for Dorian." Em tells me.

My eyebrows and nose scrunch in protest at the use of Mr. Clarke's first name.

"Get over it. I'm not calling him anything other than his first name after everything that's happened. Anyway, I tried distracting him to give you time to figure out why I was calling and get out. That's when he got suspicious, the whole 'why is a student suddenly at my house and trying to keep me from going inside' thing. Once he figured out that we knew that he had Abi, he flipped. The dude tried to go full Norman Bates dressed as Mother, I'm telling you. He ended up punching me and then slamming my head against one of the posts on the porch. It dazed me long enough for him to get inside. When I finally came to, I could hear him calling for Abi and I knew something was going on. So, I did the only thing that really made sense at the time. I grabbed a rock and threw it through a window."

Memories of Mr. Clarke in front of the closet Abi and I were hiding in and the sound of breaking glass flood in.

So that's what that noise was.

A sip from the cup is taken before I say, "How did... the cops...." I cough. Between the pressure in my head from what I assume is a concussion and dizziness from whatever pain medication they're feeding me, the sudden movement causes black dots to dance across the room. My eyes fall shut as I try to stop the urge to pass out, and it's only when I'm confident I won't that I look at them again. "How did they know to come?"

Maddi raises a half-curled hand. "That one was me. Cai was on the way to drop Casey and me off when he tried calling Em." The two exchange another look. "When she didn't answer, he got worried — well, I mean, we both did. It wasn't hard to figure out that something probably went wrong, and you guys needed help."

"But you didn't..."

Oh, this throat thing sucks.

"Know where you guys were? Once I told them what my suspicions were, they told me someone had already called and officers were on their way. It took some convincing to get Cai to actually take us home after that. He wanted to go hunt down the sirens and chase the cop cars." She tries to smile again, but there's pain behind her eyes.

Something happened.

"I must've called before her," Em cuts in. "After throwing the rock, I hid around the corner of the house and called them." She looks at Maddi then back to me.

I glance around the room, then back at them. "Where is Cai... and Casey?"

"Cai's at home," Em says. "I told him to get some rest and I'd call when you woke up. I'll do that in a minute."

"And I figured it was best for Casey to not be involved more than she needs to be," Maddi says, "so I dropped her off at my house before coming here. Besides, I thought it would be better if just family was here for now."

Family. Why would it need to be just family?

A knot forms in the pit of my stomach. "Thank you."

"You're welcome, but next time we go to the cops when *I* want to."

"Let's hope there isn't a next time," Em says in a flat tone.

"Well, right, yeah, but if there is, we go when I say it's time."

"Deal." I finish the cup of water and set it aside.

There's that heavy silence that settles in.

Man up and ask.

"What happened to Mr. Clarke? Last thing I remember...." I let my words trail off as the sinking starts to take over. Flashes of the night come back: Max charging up the stairs, Abi and Max tumbling back down them, the horrible sound her body makes when she hits the floor. It all replays over and over with the sounds in stereo.

"Mr. Clarke was arrested and charged with kidnapping and... attempted murder," Maddi says with hesitation. "The cops shot him when they found him trying to kill you, but it must not have been too damaging of a place because we saw him being taken out a few hours ago."

He was shot and survived? He should've died.

A gruesome thought, but one I don't regret.

"Is Abi up yet? Does she know? She's probably still freaked out. When can I go see her?" I look between them but pause the rest of my questions when I notice the sullen expression sitting on them. "What? Didn't they bring her here? She hit her head pretty hard."

"I'm sorry, Hunter." All sarcasm and playfulness are gone from Em's tone. This is loving Em, supportive Em — that side of my sister almost no one sees. Why is she being so sweet? All Maddi said was that Mr. Clarke was being arrested and charged for his crimes. Was that such a bad thing? That knot in my stomach twists again and I feel like I'm going to be sick. "Abi— sh-she didn't make it."

The words run through my head several times before they fully process. Once they do, I'm no longer seeing anything in front of me. My eyes are in their direction, but the focus is gone. Em is talking again, and I can barely hear her. It sounds like she's at the end of a tunnel. The pressure in my head is replaced with a light feeling that makes everything numb. There's a touch to my hand, but I can't bring myself to move or acknowledge the person or....

Am I breathing?

When I finally look at Em, I can feel it: the prickling in my eyes, the resistance against my chest, the cold shooting up my spine.

You're going through shock.

No, this isn't real. They're making a mistake. They accidentally switched the charts and think Abi is another patient. That can happen, right? I look down at Em's hand on mine, but it doesn't look like my hand anymore. I can feel her squeezing the hand to comfort me. The hand she's holding looks foreign, unfamiliar. I want Abi's hand in mine, to hear her say my name. I want anything other than this.

All at once, the floodgates finally open and weeks of suppressed worry and anxiety and fear burst through the mask I've built. I can't remember the last time someone saw me cry except for that moment in the car with Maddi a couple of weeks ago. But right now? Right now, everything in me is shattered. I am not strong or stoic or resilient. I'm fragile and tired and broken.

Tears stream down my face, my body shakes. Em is on the bed and wrapping her arms around me before I even register her movements. She holds me, rocks me, with soft, motherly shushing sounds. All I can do is cling to her as the shakes turn into trembling sobs. Every ounce of me is being ripped apart and set on fire.

Breathe.

I try, but it only causes more rapid breathing.

I hate this. I hate all of this. It's not fair! It wasn't supposed to end like this!

"But w-we found her!" I don't realize I'm yelling until Em jerks back. Guilt over scaring her mixes with the grief. "We got the proof. I got her out of the basement. I saved her. We were so close." I don't care how much talking hurts. It's nothing compared to the searing, emotional pain everywhere else.

"I know," Em kisses my temple before pulling me close again. Her cheek rests on the top of my head. "I'm so, *so* sorry."

"She can't be—It's not her. Em...." I look at my sister in desperation. All she's showing me is sorrow. She wants to take my pain away, she hates that this is how things are ending. She doesn't need to tell me. I can feel it.

A hand on my leg tells me Maddi is sitting on the bed near us. She wants to help comfort me. A second wave of guilt crashes down. Maddi is the one who lost a sister. My mind tries to figure out what it would be like if I lost Em, and the mere idea of it causes more tears.

"I'm sorry," she says.

I take her hand and pull her into the hug with Em and me.

"Me too." My hand smooths some of her hair as she succumbs to her own tears. "Me too."

This isn't just your pain, it isn't just your loss. She needs you too. You need each other.

THIRTY-FIVE

— • —

Days since Abi's death: 6

"Would anyone like to say a few words?" The priest's clerical collar is slightly askew. Mom's OCD must be going crazy.

"I would." When I get to the podium, we trade places and exchange a nod. The wood is smooth and polished and reminds me of the still-intact pieces of leather on my car's steering wheel: calming. The crowd is a mix of family, friends, and fellow students. With everyone silent and waiting for me to speak, the weight of having their attention makes my knees buckle.

Say something. Anything.

"Abi..." The casket is still waiting to be lowered. Powder blue with a cascade of pink and purple stargazer lilies laying over the bottom half. I blink away a few tears, then look back to the crowd. "Uh... if there was one thing I know, it's that Abi loved with every fiber of her being. She didn't half-ass things. She didn't start something unless she knew she could finish it, and if she didn't know going in, she forced herself to and called it a 'character building experience'."

A few people shuffle and some let out airy, tired laughs.

Mr. Perkins is in the front row. His eyes are red and swollen with dark circles deeper than when I saw him a few days ago. After I was released from the hospital, he came to the house and apologized for everything. For blaming me for Abi's desire to go to community college, blaming me as the cause of her disappearance. He even offered thanks for not giving up on finding Abi and keeping Maddi close through everything. Truth is, I've never been mad at him for it. He was angry, upset, and grieving. I can't say I wouldn't react the same way, but it was nice to hear the apologies. Mr. Perkins is a hard-ass, and he's not the nicest guy, but at least he can admit when he's wrong. I respect that.

Maddi is sitting between him and Casey holding their hands. Her eyes are just as swollen, just as puffy. It's clear she hasn't slept in days.

This whole process has been hard on them.

"I've never been the articulate one, but I guess what I'm trying to say is she wanted to make a difference in the world. She wanted to do something that left a mark. 'Don't go out of this world quietly,' she always said. 'Do something that will impact someone so when you're gone, you're immortalized through their memory.' I wish I could tell her she did that, and I hope she knows — wherever she is — that she won't be forgotten."

Someone at the back of the crowd sniffs.

I will myself to walk away from the podium and over to the casket. It's closed now, but my mind replays what she looked like during the viewing. They'd brought her hair back to that beautiful chestnut color and dressed her in one of her favorite pink shirts — spattered in paint, of course. My eyes fill with tears again, but I don't blink them away this time. They fall freely until the collar of my shirt is wet and scratchy. At some point over the last few days, I'd decided it's better to finally stop hiding what I'm feeling from everyone. Abi never wanted me to live with regrets. Part of that is not holding things in.

I'll do my best, Abs. Promise.

Weeks ago, I would've hidden behind my emotionless mask. I would've told everyone I was fine, put on a smile, and tried to comfort other people around me. No one would know that I was affected by everything that's happened, and everything I'd gone through. Being strong meant not showing how things effect me, that's what I'd always been told, but that's not true. Mr. Jenkins and Maddi are right: I'm allowed to be emotional. There's nothing wrong with it, and our loved ones can't be there for us if they aren't aware that something's wrong.

When I look at the crowd again, it's easy to find Mom, who's sniffling into an overused tissue with Em holding her free hand. Em's not crying, but there's a softness in her eyes that tells me she's proud and she understands and she loves me. Cai is next to her with a hand on Em's thigh. He's staring forward in a way that tells me he's internalizing a lot of what he's feeling. Maddi, still holding her father's and girlfriend's hands, stares at me with tears streaming down her cheeks. It brings me back to the café once again, but this time the tears are a mix of acceptance as well as grief. Abi might not be with us anymore, physically, but she's with us, she's safe, and I believe she's happy.

⁓

"Hey... Hunter." I turn to my right to find Jasper. His hair is slicked back and his shoulders are squared. He's walking taller than the last time I saw him.

"What's up?" My uninjured hand rubs at the cast now covering my left forearm. The rough texture keeps my mind busy and soothed, so the world doesn't feel too overwhelming.

You can go home soon. Just a little while longer.

I just want to curl up in bed. This is exhausting.

"I wanted to say I'm sorry all this happened. I'm... bad at words and stuff, and I know we're not close, but if you need anything...." He's staring at his shoes.

"Thanks, man." I clap a hand on his shoulder. "I appreciate that, and I'm sorry too." I let a silence settle between us before drawing in a quick breath. "I want to say sorry for how Em and I handled things with you, by the way."

"It's fine."

"No, man, it's not. You deserve more respect than that, not to mention we were wrong in accusing you. *I* was wr—"

"Yeah, but I could see how you came to the conclusion you did." Jasper averts his eyes.

He's doing that shrinking thing again.

When Jasper looks at me again, he says, "Well, if you need anything, we're here for you. We all lost someone."

"Yeah."

The silence between us is tension-filled this time.

"One thing, though. I saw you in the hallway at Abi's locker, and you were... paying your respects. But before you left, you kissed a picture. What was that about?"

"What—oh, no, I—" He huffs nervously, looks around, then back to his shoes. "I wasn't kissing a picture. There's a perfume bottle that Abi kept in her locker. I was, you know... trying to see if I could... still smell it."

My lungs pull in a deep breath before it's exhaled as a sigh. "Jasper, I'm going to say this as nicely as I can: that's weird, dude."

He shifts from one foot to the other. "Yeah... Sorry. It's a comfort thing, I guess. Like how you get happy when you smell your favorite food or when you catch a whiff of a childhood scent from a happy memory? It's... yeah."

All I can think of to do is nod before he excuses himself. There's a part of me that understands the innocence behind the gesture, but... "So weird."

Jasper's not even ten feet away when someone clears their throat behind me. Turning, I spot Officers Samson and Hughes. "Hey, guys."

"Hello, Mr. Greene," Officer Hughes says with a nod and a smile that's a little too chipper for the occasion.

"What can I do for you?" The last time I'd seen or spoken to either of them, they were questioning me at the hospital about the night at Mr. Clarke's house.

Officer Samson takes a step toward me, draws in a deep breath, and straightens his blazer. "We wanted to come over and offer our condolences. Things shouldn't have gone down the way they did—"

"No, they shouldn't have," I quip with a thin-lipped expression.

"Right, and we're fully looking into everything with Clarke."

"Did you ever find the laptop and journal?"

"Yeah," Officer Hughes says, "the laptop, journal, and your notebook were all found in the back of his bedroom closet. Based on the information we gathered from the scene, and your testimony, we're able to move forward with charges."

"I know the guy was obsessed with her and stuff, but why did all of this happen? How?"

"All we can say now is that he's being evaluated by the right people so he can get the help he needs, and the judge is setting a trial date in a couple days."

That was a long-winded way to say "you're not allowed to know."

At least Mr. Clarke's in custody. "Got it."

"We'll reach out if we have any further questions, but you take care." Officer Samson shakes my hand, I extend a small wave to Officer Hughes, and watch them head back into the crowd of departing funeral goers.

"What'd they want?" Em asks.

She and Maddi stand on either side of me as their hands take each of mine to squeeze. I squeeze theirs back while Maddi rests her head on my shoulder. It's a comfort I didn't realize I needed until now.

"Just wanted to clear their conscience about everything." She doesn't need to know they were updating me on the case yet. There will be time to talk about that later.

"Are you going to be okay?" Maddi lifts her head and turns to look at me.

"Eventually." I wrap my arm around her shoulders to pull her in for a side hug.

Maddi forces a smile. "So, what do we do now?"

"Well, I'm starving," Em blurts out.

Maddi and I look at her with matching, blank expressions.

"WHAT?" Em grins, moves so she's in between us, hooks an arm around each of our necks, and sighs dramatically. "I'm kidding. Sheesh."

"We do what she wanted. We remember her and we... try to move on. We finish the semester then the school year. Em and I go to BCC in the fall, and you attend your senior year."

Maddi scoffs and ducks her head to pull from Em's hold while her hands find her hips. "We're supposed to pretend everything's normal again?"

"No. I didn't say anything about 'normal.' I said we try to move on. It won't be easy, and it'll suck, but we helped each other through this craziness. We can help each other through whatever else life decides to throw at us next."

"Yeah, what gimpy said," Em says with a giggle.

I give Em a side glance before rolling my eyes.

She flashes a Cheshire Cat-like grin. "So... about getting food."

"Oh my god, is that all you can think about right now?" Maddi asks.

"I know a place that makes a pretty rockin' milkshake," Casey says with a gentler version of that commercial-ready smile I'd first met her with.

Em's arms gesture to Casey theatrically. "At least *someone* understands me."

With a small huff, I shake my head. "Yeah, sure, *she's* the one that understands you."

Em slaps my casted arm.

While the three of them laugh at my pained groan, Cai comes over and pulls Em against him by the waist, and I take a moment to look at them. A group of misfits that found each other and became a family. A smile slowly works onto my face as a wash of true comfort and acceptance settles over me for the first time in weeks.

"What are you smiling at, weirdo?" Em asks while resting her head on Cai's shoulder.

I shake my head slowly and say, "Nothing. Let's go get you that milkshake."

ABOUT THE AUTHOR

R.L. Bates is an author of crime based mystery-thrillers for both adults and teens. They were born in Michigan, have lived in many states throughout their life, and holds a BA in Criminal Justice and Criminology with a concentration in Forensic Psychology. When not working or writing, they can be found singing, crocheting, or visiting local haunts. To learn more about them, follow them on Twitter at @RL_Bates

ACKNOWLEDGMENTS

A hardy *thank you* to Loki for all of the love and understanding and patience that you've given me through this process, and for being my very first reader. This (quite literally) wouldn't exist if you didn't help me develop Hunter and his story. He only exists because you do, and for that, I am eternally grateful.

To my Momma, who has always supported my wild ideas. I'm sorry you didn't get a chance to read this story, but I have full faith that you were with me during every painstaking hour I've put into it.

To my wonderful Editor, Carlo, who took a chance on my story and gave it so much love and attention. I can't wait for our future collaborations.

To my Pocket Janes. You wonderful humans know who you are, and the amount of reassurance and assistance you've graciously offered me is insurmountable. Thank you for *everything*.

To every other person who offered me nothing but words of love and support, thank you. It means the absolute world to have such a thunderous circle in my corner cheering me on.